THE BAKER'S CREEK BILLIONAIRE BROTHERS SERIES

USA TODAY BESTSELLING AUTHOR
CLAUDIA BURGOA

Copyright © 2021 by Claudia Burgoa
Cover: By Hang Le
Edited by: Tori Peck
Christine Yates
Kaila Ramos
Orcas Graphic: Amanda Shepard

All rights reserved.

By payment of the required fees, you have been granted the non-exclusive, non-transferable right to access and read the text of this e-book on your personal e-reader.

No part of this text may be reproduced, transmitted, downloaded, distributed, decompiled, reverse engineered, stored into or introduced into any information storage and retrieval system, in any form or by any means, whether electronic, photocopying, mechanical or otherwise known or hereinafter invented, without the express written permission of the publisher.

Except by a reviewer who may quote brief passages for review purposes.

This book is a work of fiction. Names, characters, brands, organizations, media, places, events, storylines, and incidents are the product of the author's imagination or are used fictitiously.

Any resemblance to any person, living or dead, business establishments, events, locales, or any events or occurrences is purely coincidental.

The author acknowledges the trademarked status and trademark owners of various products, brands, and-or restaurants referenced in this work of fiction, of which have been used without permission. The use of these trademarks is not authorized with or sponsored by the trademark owners.

Sign up for my newsletter *to receive updates about upcoming books and exclusive excerpts. Want to be a part of my blogger or Instagram team, sign up today:*

→ Master Blogger List: https://geni.us/CBBloggers

→ Bookstagrammer List: https://geni.us/CBGrammers

→ Booktokers: https://geni.us/CBTiktokers

www.claudiayburgoa.com

Also By Claudia Burgoa

The Baker's Creek Billionaire Brothers Series

Loved You Once

A Moment Like You

Defying Our Forever

Call You Mine

As We Are

Yours to Keep

September 2021

Luna Harbor (2021/2022)

Finally You

Simply You

Truly You

Always You

Perfectly You

Madly You

Second Chance Sinners Duet

Pieces of Us

Somehow Finding Us

Against All Odds Series

Wrong Text, Right Love

Didn't Expect You

Love Like Her

Until Next Time

The Spearman Brothers

Maybe Later

Then He Happened

Once Upon a Holiday

Almost Perfect

My One

My One Regret

My One Despair

The Everhart Brothers

Flawed

Fervent

Found

Standalones

Us After You

Someday, Somehow

Chasing Fireflies

Something Like Hate

Until I Fall

Finding My Reason

Christmas in Kentbury

Chaotic Love Duet

Begin with You

Back to You

Unexpected Series

Uncharted

Uncut

Undefeated

Unlike Any Other

Decker the Halls

Co-writing

Holiday with You

To my father. He inspired an entire series.

"I love you without knowing how, or when, or from where. I love you straightforwardly, without complexities or pride; so I love you because I know no other way." — Pablo Neruda

Hadley's Prologue

YOU KNOW what they say about small towns: they're a little piece of real estate hell. Well, maybe saying *they* is an exaggeration. *I* am the one who says that.

I was born and raised in a hell hole called Baker's Creek. The town is a two-hour drive east from Portland, near Mount Hood. Many of its residents love it, but some of us couldn't wait to leave the place as soon as we were old enough to.

In my defense, I was the awkward kid who spent her free time in the library, worked at the ice cream parlor in Happy Springs— that's the town next to Baker's Creek—and skipped parties because I had a babysitting job lined up. Not even one I found myself, my mom scheduled them for me. I'm pretty sure that she did it so that I would skip some of the parties that happened at the old Aldridge mansion.

Anyway, due to my awkwardness, the Regina Georges of the town had a field day with me. It's to no one's surprise that the moment I received my high school diploma, I drove away and swore I'd never go back.

It was goodbye, Baker's Creek and hello, Denver.

Turns out, that I could only be away for so long. Not only am I back, but I'm working on the point of the town where everything is happening.

What's happening in Baker's Creek, you ask?

The Aldridge family is back in town.

I know, I lost you. So a little background. Legend says that the Aldridge family came to the west side of the country during the gold rush. Once they became filthy rich, they established themselves in Oregon, on the east side of Mount Hood. They own a ski lodge called The Lodge, a factory called Aldry's Sweet, and pretty much all the land.

Now that the patriarch William Aldridge is dead, his sons have moved to Baker's Creek. No one knows why they're there. As small towns go, there are several rumors like "they're here to sell the town," or "they want to increase the rent and kick everyone out of Baker's Creek." My favorite? "They came to eat the young." I don't know who is saying that one, but you have to admit that it's hilarious.

I know why they are here. I can't tell you.

I'm now aiding them with their children— *aiding*, not babysitting. If you can keep a secret, I'll say that their father left them everything under several conditions. One of them is that they can't hire anyone to help them at home. In order to be their kids' friendly babysitter, I had to sign an NDA. See why I can't mumble a word about their lives?

So, my lips are sealed. I can't say much about them, not even to

Mom. I might not be able to say anything about the brothers, but I can tell the Aldridge family everything I know about the town. I'm Aldridge's source of information when it comes to the town. What I don't know, I'll research. With my help, they might be able to uncover a thing or two about their past, their father, and the reason why they are here.

I might be broke, single, and desperate, but I'm ready to become one of the Hardy Boys, or maybe Nancy Drew– whatever I need to do to crack the case.

We're going to be digging around the town's history to find some truths behind the Aldridge family.

Mills's Prologue

I'VE BEEN SKATING ALL my life. Hockey is my passion.

I also like to collect useless statistics. They make me feel better.

People swear I'm a jock, but in fact, I'm pretty nerdy. I like to learn more than just the plays for the next game. I don't tell many people because I'm a hockey player. My fans want to know if I have hard thighs, if I get laid often, how big my dick is. You don't believe me, do you? I swear, those are the kind of questions that fans post on my social media timelines or send through direct messages. They don't care that I'm more preoccupied with statistics.

Did you know that the average family size in the world is four-point-nine people?

Or that the average number of children per family is two-point-three kids?

Did you know that the average person falls in love for the first time between the age of twelve and eighteen?

When I was young, collecting these statistics gave me more ammunition to hate my father. Thanks to him, I'm one of seven brothers—not all from the same mother. My friends while growing up all had one or two siblings max.

I was the tallest in my class.

In theory, our family size is fourteen if we count our mothers. That's ten more than the world's average. However, my philanderous father didn't tell his wife or mistresses about each other until the paparazzi caught him with one of his bastard children.

Who already has a half dozen women and yet still decides to date a famous pop star? Dear ol' Daddy who was arrogant as fuck. He was bound to get caught in the middle of some celebrity drama. None of our mothers were surprised when he finally did.

Our father divorced his wife. Our mothers got full custody of us and we only got to see dear ol' Dad once a year—along with our brothers. We were never a family, but we pretended to be close during that week. Our father never cared much about us, but when he died, he left a will that fucked up our lives. I don't have daddy issues, but I think he died trying to give them to me.

I'm always looking for mediocrity because I'm tired of the weird shit that's been happening to me since I was born. Maybe that's why, at the age of thirty-four, I've still never fallen in love.

The only person I love unconditionally, other than my mom, is my son, Arden. He's the best thing that's ever happened to me.

I don't know the statistics about single fathers, nor do I plan on looking them up. I'm just trying to be the best dad I can be. Not that I can do a great job right now while I'm stuck in Baker's Creek living with my five brothers, three sisters-in-law, a baby, and several animals.

Arden and I went from being a family of two to a family of

almost ten. My brothers are a handful. Censuring their language is fucking hard. The swear jar doesn't work—most days they throw in a hundred-dollar bill and say: "for whatever *shit* I say during the *fucking* week."

My kid learned to say "what the fuck" before he turned two. Well, it's more like 'de fug,' but that's what I'm dealing with lately. The only perks of not living in Vancouver are that my son's mother isn't nagging me about seeing our son or asking for money because she's broke.

Before you judge me, she relinquished her parental rights when I refused to marry her. It was a one-night stand. I stepped up and took charge of my baby, who I love with all my heart.

I hate drama, and yet, it follows me everywhere. I'm pretty sure there's some statistic about the average person having only enough drama to keep them preoccupied. If my life were a TV show, it'd play on TNT.

You don't believe me? Let's recap.

I live with an arrogant CEO, Henry.

A bloodsucking lawyer, who happens to be made out of shit and other stinking garbage, Pierce.

A heartthrob musician who, up until he almost died, was an undercover agent for a high intelligence security company, Beacon.

A former Ranger, Delta force, or who-the-fuck-knows-what-he-was-because-he-won't-tell-us. That'll be my brother Vance, who, in addition to bringing us his drama, brought his mercenary friends close enough that they almost killed the entire family.

Last but not least, there's Hayes, who happens to be the doctor and the most grounded of all of us. I think.

Listen. I love my brothers, but I'd give anything to have a peaceful, average life. Is that too much to ask?

Chapter One

Hadley

ONE OF THE benefits of working as a social media director for a hockey team is that you don't work on Mondays. There are a few others, like getting signed jerseys for Dad or for charities. There are a few disadvantages, though, like dealing with jocks who don't take my job seriously. They think I'm just some kind of hockey groupie—not to be confused with a puck-bunny—whose only purpose in life is to ogle at them and post pictures of them online, when really, I'm there to make them look good on social media.

Another disadvantage: after a long Saturday game, I'm so exhausted I don't even have the energy to call my friends and do something fun.

I stare at my fingernails, a freshly painted dark green. At the very least, I can pamper myself during my downtime. I even blow dry my hair instead of letting it air-dry and tying it up into a ponytail. If only Randall, my live-in boyfriend, was here, we could order take-out and have a candlelit dinner, but I have no idea where he is at the moment.

We don't see each other often. Lately, I feel like he's my roommate.

My mom has a special radar. She knows when to call me, when I'm causing trouble, or when I need some homemade cookies. The lady is wise in many ways. She lacks in others, but that's a different story. It's Sunday evening. I'm alone at home waiting for my boyfriend to come back from what he calls "work." I was working just like him, and yet, I'm here.

Today is one of those days when I wonder if our relationship still works. Other times, I believe we're meant for each other and we'll get married soon. Like last December, when I caught him browsing the Cartier website—I thought that was it, he was buying me an engagement ring.

My hopes to get a sparkly, solitaire ring vanished when he showed me his new *Cartier* watch. Listen, I'm not dying to marry the man. But, if marriage isn't the next step, what are we doing together? After three years living in the same place, we're like an old boring married couple.

Hello, I'm just twenty-eight.

Work and his family, who pretty much own him, come first. He always comes late from work. I can't even remember the last time we had sex, it was *that* long ago.

So much for dating an older guy who wouldn't be playing games and would know how to treat me. I'd happily give up our fancy Downtown apartment for a more loving relationship.

What are the alternatives?

I can push him to discuss our relationship, but my hints don't seem to land, and we only have so much time to fix it. The other option? Break up with him, move out, and probably find a job where he isn't my boss. It sucks, because I actually really love my job.

But my old college roommate, Alice, who is also a social media director for the company where she works, swears I can earn more than what I'm making right now. Even worse, she says I'm earning the same as her intern. That's pathetic. But dating the boss makes things tricky. If I ask for a salary increase, Human Resources and his family might look at it differently.

If I had known when we met that he was my boss, I would never have agreed to date him.

Would it be too crazy to suggest couple's counseling?

We're not married, but we've been living together for two and a half years. Maybe if my schedule was a regular nine-to-five, we'd see each other more often. This would be a great moment to discuss my relationship with Mom.

She might have an idea or two on how to bring my relationship back to life. She's been married to Dad for thirty-two years. She might agree that it's time to search for a new job. Unlikely, since she loves that I am a: director.

My phone rings with a call from my mother just as I'm searching for new jobs. She really is scarily perceptive.

"Hey, Mom."

"Hadley, sweetie, how are you? Your dad and I were just talking about you," she says. "I'm sorry the Troopers lost the game."

"If you ask me, they need a new coach. But Randall isn't listening."

Okay, that might be another reason why Randall is not home yet. He must be at his uncle's house discussing the game and strategizing their next move. The Denver Troopers used to be one of the best, if not *the* best, hockey teams in the league. Now, the Vancouver Orcas have taken that spot.

"How is Randall doing?"

Mom likes my boyfriend just enough. Well, more like she tolerates him, but Dad isn't a fan. When they come to visit us, Mom's always complaining about Randall. Dad barely speaks to him. He says he's an entitled asshole, but as long as he treats me right, he's okay.

If you ask anyone else who lives in Baker's Creek, they'll tell you Randall is the best boyfriend a woman could ask for. Mom likes to make up stories that are far from the truth and make me sound like the perfect daughter. Therefore, I have the perfect boyfriend too—even when she doesn't think so herself. Thanks to Mom's tales, the people in my hometown believe he's the second coming of Prince Charming and that I live a fairy tale. It's not.

It's just like any other relationship in the world. We have our ups and downs. Well, we've been in a down for a while now, but maybe in a few months when hockey season is over, we'll get back on track. Instead of brooding, I should be googling trips to the Caribbean. That's what we need: a vacation outside the city, far away from his family and work.

"He's been busy. Being the general manager for the team isn't easy. His family is demanding. I think they are going to trade a few players." The excuses I make for his absence just flow like a well-known nursery rhyme. It soothes the curiosity of others, and it makes me sound like I have everything under control.

I should tell her the truth, that I don't really know how he's doing. We barely see each other. We don't speak much, and I don't know what I should do about it.

"How's the town?" I ask instead, moving the conversation along. "Are the Aldridges still in Baker's Creek?"

"Things have been strange since that explosion," she sighs.

Mom called me a week ago, almost crying. There had been an explosion and gunshots in the Aldridge mansion. The police confirmed the blast, but they said there were never gunshots. The rumors about the brothers killing each other spread like wildfire for days up until four of them reappeared.

I won't lie, it worries me that the explosion was caused by a person and not an accident. "Mom, is there any more information about the explosion?"

"We don't know what happened. The doctor and the musician are still missing." Her voice cracks. "Some people said they died in the fire along with the bandmates. After all, it was his studio."

If that were true, the real news outlets would have reported it. There's nothing about the band Too Far from Grace circulating.

"If he is indeed dead, that'll be two Aldridge boys gone before the age of thirty. At least the rest are safe." Her voice is slightly lost. "He was a good kid. Always polite. He left good tips in the jar. I don't know what to believe, the Google says that he was on tour and he had an accident—he was drunk and fell off the stage. He is in the hospital, recuperating. I hope it is true and that he is alive."

What? I search for it right away and there it is, the news started circulating today. He was in San Diego when it happened. Interesting. So then, where is the doctor?

"I'm sorry, Mom," I whisper, instead of asking where the doctor is. "So, the town is mourning?"

"No. Most of the people just want to know what happened. They don't care if one or all of them died as long as it doesn't affect them. That is the problem. We don't know why there was an explosion. And what if we're not safe. That guy, Vance, was a soldier. If someone followed him here, they could kill the entire town."

Oh God, the conspiracy theories are crazy. It's useless to tell her that all of it is gossip, so I just say, "You're safe."

"You don't know that."

"Mom, it's Baker's Creek. You said it was a music studio, right? Maybe the construction company didn't set up the electric wires right."

"That's another problem. Easton, the new contractor, lost a lot of business because of that," she whispers. "Ever since those kids came to town, nothing makes sense. We have more tourists. The factory is going back to its golden years, and same with The Lodge."

She goes silent. So much for having Mom cheering me up.

"I hear a but," I say. "Why is everyone concerned?"

"There's that rumor going around that they're here just because William made them. As soon as they receive their inheritance, they are leaving and selling everything," she finishes, almost releasing a sob. "What are we supposed to do if they sell?"

"It shouldn't affect you. Your business is one of the most profitable. Who doesn't love your croissants, pastries, or cookies? Dad's goat products are popular. He loves to teach. If they sell the mansion, the lodge, and the factory, you should be fine."

I don't tell her that there's no way the school will be affected if the Aldridges sell their assets.

"They are my landlords. What if the new people increase the rent? I can't afford that," she says, finally letting me know what's been bothering her since the six brothers arrived in town.

If things with Randall were different, I'd offer to lend them the money to buy the properties. As of right now, I'm not sure what's going to happen between us, and I don't have much savings. Who am I kidding? I don't have any savings. My salary barely covers half of the expenses in this house. I should've kept my mouth shut when he said he'd pay for the rent when we moved in together. Sometimes being independent and self-reliant brings more problems than I care to deal with.

"Mom, you need to stop listening to gossip. If they were just waiting for their inheritance, they wouldn't have opened a medical practice. You told me they're building a hospital. There's the animal clinic. The lawyer also opened a practice. It sounds like they're settling in, don't you think?"

"Probably."

"I'm right," I say, lying through my teeth. Well, it's not a lie, but I'm just feeding her bullshit to calm her down. The Aldridges are billionaires. They can afford to open all these practices and close them just the same. If the businesses are well established, they can even sell them and make a profit. Mom doesn't need to know that.

"Other than the Aldridges, what is the town up to, Mom?"

"Mary Beth is pregnant," she says. "Her parents sent her to Portland. They said she got a job there, but we know the truth."

"One of the Marys?" I *hate* the Marys. They are the queen bees of the town, and they made sure to make my life miserable while growing up. To spice things up–and in hopes that this will circulate around town–I say, "You think one of the Aldridges knocked her up?"

"No," she says defensively. "They keep to themselves. They are like their grandmother. She always thought we were beneath her."

She might be right. But, if they're anything like me, they're just avoiding being part of the gossip. Everyone is nice and sweet until they have something good to tear you apart.

"How do you even know that she's pregnant, Mom?"

"Your aunt heard the nurse give her prenatal vitamins and a prescription. She also bought a pregnancy test in the convenience store. A week later, she disappeared," she mumbles.

Who needs to be in Baker's Creek when Mom can give me the small-town gossip experience?

"Any wedding news?" she asks, changing the conversation back to me.

"Mom, I'm not ready to get married."

"He's almost forty," she reminds me. What would she think if she knew he's divorced? "He might want to settle soon. That's why he gave you that ring."

Okay, so I told her about the time I caught Randall browsing for jewelry. She assumed he'd proposed. I said no, but he gave me a ring as a Christmas present. It was better than what actually happened, which was him forgetting to buy me something and cut me a check when I gave him a Hermes tie. I bought that ring outside the light rail train. It cost me twenty bucks, but it looks like a million-dollar piece.

"He didn't propose. It was just a gift."

"I don't understand the two of you. You've been living with him for years, and there's no commitment."

Welcome to the club, Mom.

"It's Denver, Mom. Things are different when you live in a city. Not everyone gets to marry their high school sweetheart and live happily ever after," I say, wondering if I'll ever be as happy as my parents are. "How's Dad?"

"He's well. He's currently making cheese," she says. "Since the Aldridge ladies got involved in the festival's board, he has been able to set a booth every week."

"So things are going well with his girls?"

She laughs. "Yes. I guess the investment is paying off—finally."

Dad is a chemistry and physics teacher. They don't pay him much at the high school, but he loves what he does. The day he said, "I'm buying goats so we can make cheese, moisturizer, and soap," we thought he was going crazy. Randall said, "goats might be better than a mistress." That's what his father chose to do when *he* was in the middle of an existential crisis.

Listening to Mom talking about Dad's girls and how much he enjoys his hobby makes me want to visit them. At least for the weekend. It makes me want to, but I won't.

She'll want me to bring Randall. The town will want to see my ring. They'll ask about my penthouse. (I'll remind you we have an apartment.) Mom likes to keep up with the Joneses; she brags about my life and embellishes it as she sees fit.

I can't bring my fiancé because I'm not engaged. I can't tell them about my fancy job because the only thing fancy is the title. All I can do is listen to her talk and maybe convince Randall to pay for their tickets so they can come to Denver.

Maybe I need to work on our relationship. I'll get us back to a happy place, and then maybe we can work on a proposal and a better salary because, even if we get married, I want my independence.

Is this even possible?

Are Randall and I even meant to be together? Do I want to marry him?

Just as I hang up with Mom, he calls.

"Hi," I greet him. "Should I order takeout?"

"Nah, I'm having dinner with my parents. You should order something for yourself. Use my credit card. It's in my office," he says, clearing his throat. "So, listen, Suzie called."

My eyes close as I feel the chill of his words sipping through my body. Why is he mentioning his ex-wife? I ask the obvious, "Your Suzie?"

"Yeah," he clears his throat. "She's moving back from New York, and her parents want me to help her search for a new place. Since we need to find it soon, my cousin Tyler is helping. I might stay with him tonight."

I understand that Tyler lives close to the foothills, but why is he staying with him? Hoping I don't sound too needy, I ask, "Are we okay, Randall?"

"What kind of question is that, babe?"

The kind you ask when you barely see your live-in boyfriend and he chooses to spend Sunday with his family searching for a house for his ex, I want to yell, but I don't.

"I haven't seen you this weekend. We haven't been on a date for months. Two more weeks without sex, and I might be re-virginized."

He laughs. "Leave it to you to make up shit like that. We're fine. You've been busy learning the new social media platforms and making the guys look good even when they suck. I'm trying to figure out a way to make them suck less. It's temporary. Once the season is over, we'll go back to normal."

I sigh with relief. He's right. I'm just being paranoid.

"See you tomorrow?"

He chuckles in response. "Sure, babe. I'll try to move my schedule so we can at least have lunch together, okay?"

"Sounds like a plan."

"Love you, babe," he says and doesn't wait to hear it back.

Chapter Two

Mills

"DADA!" A voice booms inside my head. The sound feels like a rubber band bouncing in my mind as I go from deep sleep into a groggy state of reality.

When I open my eyes, I see my darling son jumping on the bed frantically, yelling, "Dada, Dada, Dada!" about a hundred times per second.

Kids are precious, they said. You'll cherish every second you have with them, they said.

It makes me wonder if every person who has children blocks out the sleepless nights, the tantrums, and the tiny feet bouncing on the bed while you're trying to get some sleep.

I love my son, he's the best part of me. But I miss sleeping.

Two more fucking minutes, I want to beg, but instead, I heave myself out of bed.

I can't remember the last time I slept more than five hours in a row. This kid is slowly killing me. I can already read the headlines: *Former Hockey Player Dies From Lack of Sleep.*

No. That can't be true. I won't become a former player, I'm just thirty-four. Next year, I'll be back on the ice. My knee is almost as good as new. The eighteen-month sentence to live in Baker's Creek is over by the end of November. I just need to find a team that'll take me since the Orcas released me from my contract.

"Dada, baffes."

"Wa-ffles. Not baffes," I correct him, lifting him from the bed and flying him around the room. "Ready for takeoff. Next stop, the kitchen!"

He giggles with excitement. We both imitate the noise of a plane engine as we go down the stairs.

I stop when we spot Easton, the contractor, measuring the railing. "Isn't it a little early for house visits?"

He looks at me and shakes his head. "Henry texted me last night to make sure I'd arrive early."

"You're the only person who puts up with him," I pat his shoulder as I continue descending the stairs. "Say hi to Mr. Rodin, Sport."

"Hi," Arden grins and waves his hand.

"So, what are you doing with the stairs?" I ask.

Beacon finally woke up from the induced coma and, according to Hayes, he could be flying back home as early as tomorrow or as late as six weeks. He sent more instructions to Henry, who has been making changes to the house and calling every person he knows to order what our little brother needs to recover.

"We're adding a stairlift so Beacon can go up and down the stairs. It's faster than adding a room to the downstairs area."

I huff. "I bet you want to press ignore every time we call you."

"No. Currently, you're my only customer. Half of the town thinks it was my fault that the studio exploded," he mumbles.

"Sorry about that. That might give you some time to finish my ice rink," I grin and then leave him to his work.

My brother Pierce is in the kitchen, and he smiles at Arden. "How are you this morning, Sport?"

"Otay," Arden answers.

"Did you have a good night's sleep?" He says, taking him from my arms.

Arden gives him a sharp nod and says, "Baffes."

"You need to teach him how to say eggs." Pierce gives me a look that says, *we can't keep eating waffles.*

I had to agree. It's been his favorite breakfast since the last time Beacon was here, and for the past three weeks, he's been looking for Beacon and waffles. We can give him the waffles but not his favorite uncle.

Beacon and Arden have a pretty tight bond. My little brother has been there for us since he learned that he would be an uncle. Beac and his girlfriend, Grace, visited us often. Now that we live in Baker's Creek, he's used to seeing his favorite uncle every day. His current absence is messing him up a lot.

"Any news from Beacon?"

"Vyk!" Arden claps.

Pierce gives me my son back and begins to pull out all the ingredients to prepare the waffles.

"Hayes hasn't called with the morning update." He shrugs. "You should focus your energy on finding someone to help us with the little ones. Blaire is about to pop, and she won't be able to help us with Carter and Arden."

"Who is going to want to work for us without getting paid?" I ask. We'd have to find a descendant from Mother Teresa if we want someone to help us for free.

Not even my mother wants to come and help me with my son.

"Can you just try?" Pierce insists.

"It's impossible. What am I supposed to offer in exchange for twenty to thirty hours of babysitting a week? If we wait until summer, there might be a few teenagers willing to do it for some change. But still, it wouldn't be free."

He looks me up and down. "You could always offer your body," he says with a laugh "We can use you as a stallion. Are you any good?"

If I could, I'd flip him off or curse him out. However, the two-year-old begging for *baffes* stops me from doing it.

"Har, har," I say, trying to control my temper. "Why can't we have an adult conversation?"

"We could, but it'd be boring." He shrugs. "We should find someone who needs legal help, housing, and maybe eggs."

He points to the nearly overflowing basket of fresh eggs he's collected from his chickens. Another reason why we should be eating eggs and not just waffles. "Beacon spoiled us," I sigh.

When it was his turn to cook, he made frittatas, omelets, muffins, crepes…it's like living in a five-star restaurant where you get the best breakfast in town. The days he didn't have to cook, he'd still make Arden whatever he chose.

"As I said the other day, if we set up a childcare facility in the factory, we could hire people." I remind him of the brilliant idea I had a few months ago that everyone keeps shutting down.

"Listen, Sparky, as much as that sounds great for the employees, it doesn't help me. It'd be ridiculous to drive my son to Happy Springs every morning when I work here. Leyla and I need someone to watch him for a few hours."

"Ah, this is about you, isn't it?"

He glares at me. "I'm not in the mood to deal with you. Just keep looking for someone who might need this job."

For the sake of my kid, I don't continue the conversation.

A few seconds later, Blaire is running down the stairs. "I need someone to drive me to Oregon." She touches her swollen belly and winces.

"Vance can fly you," I offer, looking at her hospital bag. "Why? Are you having the baby?"

She nods. "I am. Hayes is not here and I need a doctor."

Pierce shakes his head and pulls out his phone. "I'll take care of the doctor on call." He points at me. "You call *him*."

I do as he says, and call Hayes right away.

"Yeah?" My brother answers.

"Your wife is in labor."

"Don't call Hayes. He's busy with Beacon," Blaire scolds me.

I give her an oops-I-forgot shrug. It's better than, 'your husband told us to call him when this happened.' He knew she'd demand to go to Portland.

"I'll make a few calls. You guys know what to do, right?"

"Yes, we do. Safe travels," I say, hanging up.

"Why did you do that?"

"We're taking you to your practice. Everything is ready there. He'll be home in just a couple of hours."

"What if something happens and he's not here?" She's almost choking with tears.

Blaire is a strong woman, but she's been going through hell. Even when we've been trying our best to be there for her, she misses Hayes a lot. I take her into my arms and say, "Everything is going to be okay."

She places a hand on her back and winces. "I'm trying not to be scared."

"Nothing is going to happen, and he'll be here before the baby arrives," I promise her.

Pierce calls everyone, and the house is not only awake but full of chaos.

I might complain about how crazy things are in this house, but I like knowing that my son is growing to have a somewhat normal childhood because of them. It's no longer just me and the occasional visit from my mother or Beacon. I'm trying to give my son what I didn't have, an average family life.

Chapter Three

Mills

A WEEK after Machlan Carter Aldridge is born, I'm already itching to leave the house. My new nephew is adorable, but just like all newborn babies, he is demanding. Arden is having trouble falling asleep and I'm not sure if it's because he's missing Beacon or because Carter and Machlan wake up every two seconds. Living with two newborns is probably the closest thing to hell. I'm not looking forward to having Henry's twins around.

I wonder if his wife, Sophia, can stay pregnant for another six months.

At least with Hayes back in the house, the chaos diminishes slightly. Still, the weight of everything that's happened makes it hard to breathe sometimes.

There are too many uncertainties. Even though Hayes believes that Beacon will walk again, he can't guarantee that one-hundred percent. After the explosion, almost losing Beacon, and killing his ex-boyfriend, our brother Vance is a mess. He's always kept to himself, but now he doesn't talk to us at all. We only know he lives in the house because we have to share all our meals. If Beacon were here, he'd be following him around and making him talk.

None of us are like Beacon.

Since today is my day off, I decided to drive to Portland. Arden and I need some alone time, and I need to skate. Pierce lets me borrow his SUV. Arden and I are walking toward the garage, when a man wearing an Orcas cap walks toward us.

Did someone let a fan know I live here?

I try not to panic. I wouldn't be surprised if I have a stalker, but a stalker who has the code for the iron gate? That's impossible. I look toward the lake to see if there are any security guards left. Beacon's boss left a couple of men to keep an eye on the property until he knew we were safe. There's no one there.

The beauty of this land is that we're surrounded by trees, the lake, and the barn. Unfortunately, we also discovered that all of these acres leave many places for a bunch of mercenaries to hide for days without being seen.

"Good morning, Mills and Arden," he greets us.

Arden waves back at him. I narrow my gaze and realize it's Darren Russel, one of the doctors who treated Beacon and the new neurosurgeon that'll work with Hayes. I'm still skeptical about his presence. Who needs a neurosurgeon in a small town?

He stares at my duffle bag. "Where are we going?"

"Arden and I are heading to Portland."

He smirks. "Goody. I love Portland, and I need to go there. I was hoping that one of you would lend me a car. But if you are going, we could go together and save on fuel. What do you think, Arden?"

My son looks at him, and then at me, and smiles.

"I love this kid. He's always smiling." He looks around and whispers. "And he doesn't cry, unlike the other two."

"You didn't have to deal with Arden's infant years. They weren't easy." I hate to be brusque, but I need to leave and he's blocking my escape., "Sorry, but we're heading out."

He looks at me confused. "And here I thought the grouchy one was the military guy." He gives me a playful look. "Or do you have a problem because I am…hot?"

I ignore him. He doesn't know us at all. If he lived here, he'd understand or would want some solitude as well. I need to be far away from my family and anyone who has anything to do with this town. Is that too much to ask?

"It's not you. I'm trying to have a day away from my brothers and this mess," I explain, making sure that he knows I'm not interested in his advances.

He nods as if he understands my conundrum. "What if I promise to be quiet?"

I laugh and that's the moment when Vance steps outside the house. "I heard you're going to Portland. Do you need me to fly you?"

I look at the neurosurgeon and say, "You should be flying with him. He'll appreciate that you're hot."

"He can't handle me," Darren answers, taking off his sunglasses and winking at Vance. "Wanna give it a go?"

Vance rolls his eyes and focuses his attention on me. "I can fly *you*. I don't have anything to do today."

He wants to get away too, but I'm not his get-out-of-jail-free card.

"We need a car," I retort, trying to wiggle my way out of this situation. He can fly with Darren.

"Wonderful," Darren says, having been waiting patiently for his turn. He points a finger in Vance's direction. "He has a helicopter and a car. We're set. It would be wiser if we cut the traveling time and enjoy our time in Portland."

Ugh, I hate people who look at the practical, logical, and more sensible solution. I need to get the fuck out of this town without my brothers. But he's right about one thing. Arden will be better if we fly.

Vance gives me his best annoyed look. "He has a point."

I take a moment to think about his offer. Maybe he doesn't want to be alone. In the end, I agree. If nothing else, I can convince them to join me in the rink. Maybe they can watch Arden for ten minutes while I speed skate. I miss skating so fucking much. What are a few hours with my brother and a haughty neurosurgeon?

OUR TRIP to Portland is better than I anticipated. I hate to admit it, but including Darren, or "Dare" as he likes to be called, makes a big difference. He keeps Vance on his toes and helps me a lot with Arden while I skate by myself. He sits by the bench playing with Arden's plushy Orca. During lunchtime he convinces him that broccoli is yummy.

I let the man lie. If he can make my son eat vegetables, the guy is more than okay in my book. While Vance drives us back to the airport, Dare tells me he has a three-year-old niece who he babysits when her parents need a break. Maybe Hayes convinced him to move to Baker's Creek so he can help us take care of the kids. I doubt he'll have any patients.

We arrive at home around eight. For the first time since Machlan came home, Arden is asleep, even before his nine o'clock bedtime. Between the newborn baby, Beacon not being home, and everyone's stress, he hasn't been able to fall asleep on time. I skip his bath and just change him into his pajamas. One day without his night routine won't affect him.

I set up the baby monitor and head downstairs, catching Vance as he enters the house.

"So he made you drive him home, huh?" I ask, trying not to laugh.

"Not only that, he made me walk him to his door," he grunts. "Someone has to tell him that I'm not available."

"You could do it," I say. "Just tell him you got out of a serious relationship that ended up." I pause for effect. "Deadly."

Vance glares at me. "You're not Beacon. He might've said something funny. You're just an idiot impersonating him. And no, it's not because of Bennett. I'm just not in a good place to date. He and I were just friends with benefits."

I wave away his excuses and head to the kitchen for a six pack. "Do you want to hang out on the patio?"

It's a simple request, but it's something Beacon and I usually do together. Sometimes others will join us, like his bandmates, but it was a rare occasion for our other brothers to be there.

"Do you think we should build a covered patio around the firepit?" Vance asks, pointing at the old castle-style fire pit that we built almost a year ago.

This land was abandoned. Now, the house has a new stucco exterior the color of the sand. Pierce is building a house on the far west side of the lake, opposite of Hayes. Not that he can live there. According to the stipulations of my father's will, no one can live outside of the main house for eighteen months.

As Vance starts the fire, I ignore his question and say, "Dare is fun." We don't need to do another do-it-yourself project. Not with all the chaos happening in the house.

I wish I could see his face when he retorts, "He's annoying."

"You laughed for the first time since the explosion. Maybe for the first time since we moved to Baker's Creek. I haven't seen you have so much fun since we were children."

We made this a fun day for everyone. Even when we had to buy a few things for Dare's place, we still went to the ice rink where he flirted a lot with Vance. Then, we went for lunch, where Dare paid and called it a date.

He shrugs. "You shouldn't have invited him to have dinner with us this Sunday."

"The guy doesn't know anyone in town. It's not like I set you up to go on a second date," I laugh. "Three more, and you get lucky."

If glares could kill, I'd be dead right about now. "Darren isn't my type."

"Why?" I ask with a smirk. "Because he's not a sociopath trying to kill your family?"

Vance chuckles. He actually chuckles. And here I was worried that it was too soon to make that joke. Did he swap personalities while we were out?

Was it the air in Portland, the hour we spent teaching him how to skate on ice, or Darren Russell?

"One more stupid comment about the doctor and I'll kill you," he threatens me.

I open my beer and take a seat. "You could date one of the Marys," I tease him.

"I heard you're the father of the unborn kid. Don't you have any restraint, Mills?"

"Fuck you!" I give him the finger.

He grins. "You started it."

"Honestly, I feel bad for Mary Beth. If she's pregnant, that's going to be like having a scarlet letter sewn into her clothing. If she's not...why did she leave town?"

Vance groans. "God, we're starting to sound like everyone else in this town. Why do we care about other people's business?"

"We don't, but I worry about her. Being a single parent is hard. I didn't live in a small town, but my life since Arden's mom got pregnant is in every tabloid, social media outlet, or internet article. You can see the evolution of Mills Aldridge's road to parenting on any of them. Everyone had an opinion about my relationship with his mother, a relationship that didn't even exist. They criticized me for not marrying her, while others supported me. It's exhausting to be under the scrutiny of so many people."

Vance glances at me. "I didn't see it that way, but you're right. I wish I had been there for you."

"In no way am I judging her," I continue, ignoring his regret.

That's easily the most used phrase in this household. We all wished we had been there for each other, but we can't fix the past, can't we?

"So, why didn't you share custody of Arden with his mom?"

This is so unlike Vance. He's never been one for talking, especially talking about feelings, so I take advantage of this moment. I tell him about Margaret, Arden's Mom. The bad choices that led me to the best thing in my life, my son.

"There's always a group of puck bunnies who follow the team to every game. I didn't think much of her; I'm ashamed to admit that those fans are the easiest lay. So, I slept with her a couple of times. The condom broke during one of those times. I suggested we get the morning after pill but she said she was on the pill."

"Let me guess," Vance says. "She wasn't."

I shrug because who the fuck knows. "I'm sure you think I'm an idiot for believing her, and you're right. She was about sixteen weeks pregnant when she figured it out. She wanted me to marry her."

"I take it that you didn't want to marry an almost stranger."

"Exactly."

I skip the part where I requested a paternity test. After all, we weren't exclusive. Doing the right thing in that situation is subjective. Margaret wanted me to marry her. I wanted to take care of the baby. When she said she wanted to get rid of the baby, we agreed that she'd carry him full term and rescind her parental rights. It was easy until it wasn't. She keeps coming back trying to get into my good graces, and if all else fails. She cuts to the chase and asks for money.

"Has Arden met her?"

I shake my head. "No. I want to keep it that way. What would I even say? 'Here's the woman who doesn't want to deal with you?' He deserves better."

"Good for you," he agrees. "Our children deserve better than what our parents did for us. I still don't know why William wanted to have so many children, but never cared for us. What was the point?"

My guess is that maybe it was a way to tell our grandfather, look, the fortune will be split into seven. Not just one child who'll own it all. I don't voice it out. There are too many theories about our father's behavior to add yet a new one.

We stay quiet for a while, nursing our beers. "Do you think maybe Dad was in love with someone from the town?" I ask eventually.

"I'm not going to think about the conspiracy theories you all have. I don't care why he decided to leave me stranded here. I hate him even more because of that. If he hadn't done it, Beacon wouldn't be in the hospital." The bitterness in his voice is more sour than the beer.

Is it just Beacon or is he also thinking about his boyfriend? "You wouldn't have killed Bennett," I say, trying to coax him into talking.

If I had to kill my ex, I'd be emotionally destroyed.

"I would rather not speak about it," he mumbles, giving me an annoyed glance.

Will he ever speak to anyone but his counselor about what happened that night or the events that led to it?

"Are you still seeing a therapist?"

He nods. "It's not because I miss him. I'm angry at myself for being such an idiot. I was involved with an organization that killed innocent people just for kicks—"

"You focused on your job," I say, cutting him off. "If you had been in charge of the contracts, you would've worked for different people."

He bobs his head a couple of times, staring at the fire. "So, I'm not great with kids," he says, changing the subject a hundred and eighty degrees. "But whenever you need help with yours, I'm here."

"Look at you. It's like we're bonding," I joke.

This is the longest conversation I've had with Vance since we moved to Baker's Creek a little over ten months ago.

I hear Henry's voice before I see him, "Can we join you?"

"As long as you bring the single malt," Vance answers.

Henry shows us a bottle of Macallan 25 and glasses. "I even brought your two brothers with me."

A few hours ago, I was ready to leave town and say fuck the will and the people in the town. Right now, I'm glad I have this bunch of assholes.

Chapter Four

Hadley

IN HINDSIGHT, I should have been a little more worried when Randall said, "Suzie is coming back to Denver."

Suzie, his ex-wife. The love of his life—according to his mother — and the only woman his family approves of.

How can he be speaking to a woman who cleaned him out after the divorce, and according to him, cheated? My blood boiled with anger each time he spoke about her. It didn't bother me when he first mentioned her that fateful Sunday. All I thought was, he's going to help her look for a house.

Furthermore, I should've asked questions when he was arriving late from work, having meetings outside the office, and receiving phone calls at odd hours of the night.

I think there was a part of me — deep, *deep* down— that knew this was happening. That's the only reason I have for why I'm not surprised to find Randy thrusting deep into Suzie, splayed out on his desk as she begs for it.

Maybe I'm in shock. It's the only reason I have for why I can't look away from the little porn show. So much for bringing him lunch to the office and trying to have an impromptu date.

"Give it to her, boss," one of the executives says whistling as he cheers for him.

I finally look around me and realize that I left the door open. Like in every office, everyone breaks for gossip. This one isn't just any kind of office gossip. It's the juicy one with live action porno.

His assistant, Norma, says, "Sorry, Hadley. I had no idea—"

"You should've been at the locker rooms last night. They were going at it heavy," someone else interrupts her.

I gawk at the scene. He hates PDA and he was boning his ex in the locker room? Who is this guy?

A flash of anger blooms in my chest. This isn't a one-time situation. He's been fucking his ex-wife without caring if anyone sees him.

"So, you've been cheating on me?" I finally speak.

I'm angry with myself. Why didn't I see this coming? Everyone else seems to know about his affair. And if I'm honest with myself, maybe I just didn't care anymore, because things were bad before Suzie came back around. Maybe that's why I've been searching for a new apartment and a new job, without saying anything to my now ex-boyfriend. Still, at least I planned to attempt a conversation, like civilized people who talk about their issues and agree to break up.

At least I didn't cheat on him.

"Oooh, we should upload this on YouTube," someone says from behind me, tearing me from my thoughts.

And you know what? He's right. This show *should* be aired online. We should at least share a few pictures with the fans; everyone should know what kind of asshole their general manager is.

Randall looks over his shoulder, his eyes wide. "Fuck, Hadley, close the door."

"Oh, you need privacy? You should've thought about that before doing it in the office without locking the door." I snap a picture of them. "How will this look in the team's social media account?"

He pulls out of Suzie, turns around, and threatens me with a small chubby finger. "Put that phone down."

I snap another picture. "I can't take you seriously like that. At least pull up your pants."

"I'm sure you can find someone with a better cock," his assistant whispers to me. "He's definitely trying to make up for what he lacks in that department."

I burst into laughter. Using a picture editing app, I put the pictures in one graphic so they can easily be posted to the team's stories on each social media site.

"Hashtag," I say pettily as I type, "GM having fun."

"Hadley," he warns me again, pulling up his pants and fixing his shirt. "Put that phone down."

"Hashtag, cheater-for-life," I continue.

"I swear if you post that—"

"Aw, what are you going to do *Randy*, break up with me?" I sound sad and almost teary, but I'm just fucking angry. "We are so over, Randall. You're like a pair of worn-out shoes. They look ugly, their soles are nearly gone, but I keep using them because I don't have the energy to buy a new pair."

I feel his assistant resisting the urge to high five me.

"Do not post that or you're fired," he orders.

"Oops," I say, touching the tips of my fingers to my lips. "I already posted it."

"You are fired!" He shouts. His cheeks turn red with rage.

"Oh, no. You don't get to fire me. I quit and we," I pause to shoot a glare at the still naked woman on his desk. "We are over."

I storm away from the scene. My head is about to explode with anger, sadness, and worse, the uncertainty of what's going to happen next. Randall barges right behind me. I swear if he comes too close I'm going to use my self-defense training on him. I'll give him at least a bloody nose.

"Hadley, give me the team's social media logins. You can't possibly think that posting my privates on social media is right. We can get fined."

"I blurred your ass, your dick, and her tits." I say, finally looking up at him. "She has a nice rack, no wonder you keep offering to upgrade mine. How much did that cost you?"

"Stop," he commands. "Keep Suzie away from this fight."

I laugh derisively. "I'm just wondering, did Suzie come back or did you call Suzie?"

He ignores me and asks, "Do you know what that's going to do to the team's reputation?"

"I'm busy," I say, ignoring him right back. I know I'm being petty, but I don't have it in me to care.

He paces around the office. He halts right in front of me and says, "Hadley, what you did was childish."

I throw the last frame I have on top of my desk in the box. This is the last item that ties me into this office and the team. It's over, not only with Randall, but with a job that was fun but didn't have anything else to give me. Then, I finally feel calm enough to look at him without wanting to claw his eyes.

"Stop it. I'm sick and tired of your, 'act your age,' bullshit." I spit, jabbing my finger in his face. "This is the behavior of a woman who just found her boyfriend of three years bare ass naked fucking another woman. I have feelings. You don't get to dictate how I behave or what I feel. Not before and definitely not now. What you did is called *cheating*. If you wanted to break up with me, you could've just said, 'it's over.' You are the one who needs to start behaving like an adult."

His nostrils flare. Randall hates when he's told that he's a man child, which he is. It bothers him but he doesn't do anything to fix it. The guy would be no one without his family's money—and jobs. He's too tied up in them to even consider our relationship as more than some fling with a twenty-something-year-old woman. This is part of my latest reflections and realizations. Our relationship was a dead end. I knew it was over, of course I did. But, because I cared about him, I was trying to work things out or make our separation painless for both of us.

Clearly he never cared enough about me.

"It wasn't my intention to hurt you," he says, looking toward the closed door. "Suzie and I–we have a history together. You can't compare a marriage with what you and I have. We were different."

"What *did* we have, Randall?"

He stares at the floor.

"I thought it was a committed relationship. Three years living together. That's a lot more than just having a fling." I'm furious about this situation. What the hell man? I don't want to know anything about Suzie, and yet, I still find myself blurting out, "Do you still love her?"

Why am even I asking that? It's not like I'm in love with him. This is college all over again. I dated a guy for a couple of years and, when we graduated, he went back to Oklahoma to marry his high school sweetheart.

"It's complicated," he responds and I want to punch him on behalf of Suzie and myself.

We deserve better than a man like him. "For fuck's sake, you're almost forty. Own your actions and your emotions."

I grab my haphazardly packed box with an angry sigh. "Goodbye, Randall. It'll take a week or so to figure out where I'm going to live. Stay with your cousins, your parents, or wherever you've been sleeping with *her*."

"I'm confused," he says with hesitation. I come to a halt, and look over my shoulder. "Why don't you wait until I work through what's happening to me?"

I pivot and glance at him, wondering what else there could possibly be to think about when he's obviously moved on. "What does that mean?"

"I care about you. Why don't you stay at least until I get someone to cover your position?

I blink a couple of times at the sheer audacity of what he just said.

"You're priceless," I say with a bitter laugh.

He's confused? I'm sure once he secures another social media director the confusion will dissipate. I might be younger but I wasn't born yesterday.

"At least, give me the login information for the social media account. We need to do some damage control."

Ah, so that's why he was sugarcoating everything. I grin. "Remember that time when I proposed to hire an intern?"

He nods.

"If you had an intern, you wouldn't need the login information from me. Unfortunately for you, you ignored my suggestion. And even more unfortunate, I'm petty." I walk away with my chin up and a big smile.

He didn't take anything away from me *and* I got to have the last laugh. His uncle is probably going to fire his ass or demote him. Not to mention, the fit his mother will have when she finds out that there's a naked picture of him on the internet is going to be perfect. It's such a shame that I won't get to watch it all happen.

"Hadley!" He calls after me as I walk toward the exit. "Take that fucking picture down or you'll regret it."

"Afraid that your boss might find out what you do in your office?" I ask, not slowing down a bit.

I'm enjoying this as much as I enjoyed my last vacation in Puerto Vallarta. If only I had a piña colada to celebrate the moment.

"Goodbye, Randall."

"What happened to your motto, don't be an asshole?" He calls, in a last-ditch effort to stop me. I ignore him and step through the automatic doors to breathe in the fresh air, the sunshine, the roar of cars on I-25.

"My family is going to fire me," is the last thing I hear as the sliding doors close behind me.

Chapter Five

Hadley

IT'S OFFICIAL. My life is over.

I might as well dig a hole right next to the swings, crawl inside, and die there.

Who wouldn't want to die in a park?

This is no ordinary park. It has two sets of swings, three types of slides, and two sizes of monkey bars. The evergreens surround the playground all year long. When the snow coats the ground, it looks like an enchanted wonderland.

My life might be over but at least I'm in one of my favorite places.

The last thing I wanted to do was to come back to Baker's Creek, and yet, here I am. Sitting on the swings like I used to do during high school when I was done with homework and I couldn't sleep.

This place used to be the happiest in the world when I was a kid. When Mom closed the bakery in the afternoon, she'd bring me to the park so I could play. It was usually around supper time, so the park was empty. I could swing without waiting for my turn, and sometimes I even got to play with Mom. We would slide together several times and laugh without a care in the world.

Life was so much simpler back then. I wasn't aware that the town where I lived held more dangers than the wilderness. Here in Baker's Creek, it is eat or be eaten.

I stop swinging when I notice a man chasing a small child who's running toward me. A man running in my direction takes me out of my own head, and I stop swinging when I notice the small child he's chasing.

When he sees me, the little boy looks up and says a hopeful: "Mama?"

The sad voice liquifies my heart. I hop out of the swing in order to squat down to his level. "Hadley. My name is Hadley. What is your name?"

His adorable green eyes look at his shoes. Did he lose his mom? Maybe she died and he's still hoping to find her. My heart breaks open.

"How many times have I told you not to run—or to talk to strangers?" The man who I assume is his father chides him. "You could get lost or worse, they could take you away from me."

I glance at his father. He glares at me with suspicion and disdain, moving to put himself between me and his kid.

The kid looks up at his dad and says, "Haley," pointing at me.

"Exactly, Hadley. What's your name?"

"Awden," he answers, with a boyish grin and baby voice. I can feel the sweetness of this kid turning me into a puddle of goo.

"Nice to meet you!" I say, delighted. I shake his hand and then straighten up to talk to his dad.

"He shouldn't be talking to strangers," the man grumbles at me, cutting me off before I can say anything.

Is he seriously reprimanding me?

Just because he's almost a foot taller than I am, his broad, muscular shoulders make him look like Thor—or Charlie Hunnam —, and he has a deep husky voice. Does he think I'm going to be intimidated?

Well, someone should teach him a lesson or two on manners and maybe parenting. Can he talk to his son in age-appropriate sentences? How about not bringing him to the park so late at night?

"Keep your tone down," I say, using my mom's low-disappointed-angry tone. The woman never yelled at me but that voice made me feel worse than any spanking my father gave me when I let the goats out or broke something in the house. "He's just a baby. He confused me with his mom."

The little boy pulls my long skirt. "I wanna swin, peas?"

I pretend to look at my watch, eyeing my bare wrist playfully. "Looks like it's time for me to go home. I'm sure your dad will be happy to do it."

My heart breaks all over again as his eyes fill with tears and his lip trembles.

I look up at his dad, who is staring at us with pure panic. This man—an easy 6'4 or 6'5— looks ready to bolt, and I can't help but wonder why.

"If you allow it, I could stay for a few more minutes," I offer.

The man ignores me as he stares at his son. After a couple of seconds, he picks up the toddler, and sets him on the chair swing. Okay, he's going to do it. Even though the kid is adorable, it's best if I leave.

As I wave goodbye, the kid says, "Howdy, peas."

I look at the man and stifle a grin as he sighs harshly. "Five minutes," he says.

Gently, I push the small boy. Since it's already dark and only the moon and the stars are here to witness, I start to sing him Twinkle, Twinkle Little Star. I smile into the song as his little voice joins me. I'm not sure how long it takes but I notice his head falling slightly and his voice losing strength.

"Maybe he's ready for bed?" I stop the swing. The man picks up the little boy, whose name I'm sure is not "Awden" and says thank you.

I shrug. "It was nothing. Was he having trouble falling asleep?"

The guy nods twice. "It's been a hard couple of weeks for him."

I haven't been in Baker's Creek in years. There's no way for me to know if he's new in town or if he's from Happy Springs and he's here just visiting. Maybe he moved to Baker's Creek after his wife died. So, I say, "Change is hard."

Mom has been keeping me up to date on everything that's happening in this town since the Aldridge family came back. They've hired new people from out of town to work at The Lodge and at Aldry's Sweets, the factory they own in Happy Springs.

He probably came seeking a new life. It'd make sense why he was so defensive. He's from some big city where strangers can be in fact dangerous. Denver is a big city but I barely spoke to my neighbors. I forgot my cell phone at Washington Park and never found it. Here, people know your name and your business. They talk about each other, but they also take care of each other. If I lose a hair pin, they'll drop it by the lost and found box in the church. It's weird but that's what small towns are all about.

"Is there anything I can do to help? I could find him a playdate or..." I shrug.

He shakes his head, looking at me for a couple of seconds before he leaves.

"You're welcome, asshole," I mumble.

Yep, he's definitely from some big city where people don't have manners—like New York. I lived there for almost ten years and I never heard anyone saying thank you after I did a kind thing for them.

Once the silhouette of the man carrying the sleepy boy disappears, the park feels empty and I figure it's time to go home. Unfortunately, unlike other twenty-nine-year-old women who get to head to their own house, I'm walking back to my parent's place.

As I said, my life is over.

I have about two hundred dollars in my bank account, a pissed-off cheating ex-boyfriend who is threatening to sue me, and I'm back living with my parents.

Can you say, winner?

Me neither.

Come tomorrow, I'm going to be all the talk of the town and the social pariah.

Woohoo.

Chapter Six

Hadley

BAKERS' hours are not for everyone.

I would know. My family has owned The Cookie Jar since the beginning of the last century. The best bakery in the Northwest—maybe the country.

Ever since I was young, my mom would leave the house at three in the morning. My dad was the one who would wake me up in the morning, make sure I got ready for school, and send me on my way. I'm reminded of those days when I hear my mom moving around in her room. It's almost three in the morning when I glance at the clock, and I change my clothes to join her. Not like I can sleep much anyway.

When I arrived from Colorado yesterday, we spent the evening discussing Dad. I still can't understand why she didn't tell me how bad his accident had been. There's a big difference between: "Your dad was in an accident but he'll be fine" and arriving home to find out that he's been in the hospital for the last couple of weeks.

"Hey, Mom," I greet her, while searching for my phone. I came in late last night and left it somewhere in the living room. Maybe the dining room?

As I walk toward the kitchen where she's preparing her coffee. I kiss her cheek. She smiles at me and asks, "At what time did you come back last night?"

"Early?" I say, distracted.

I don't know what defines late or early for her, but that answer is as good as any other. I find my phone soon after, tucked in the cupboard next to the glasses. I lift it in a wave, a little sheepish. I guess I left it there when I came to drink some water.

Mom cocks an eyebrow, a familiar expression that means *Hadley can't keep track of her things*. She's partially right. I still misplace items around the house but it's been a couple of years since I declared anything lost forever. That's an improvement, right?

"Did you see your friends?" She asks.

Oh, my sweet mother who believes I have friends in Baker's Creek. The few friends I've made are either in Portland or far away from here. We're the smart ones who didn't want to stay in this prison forever.

I'm not being held here against my will, but how can I leave when Dad has a broken back and they're struggling to make ends meet? Since I can't lend them money, I moved in with them so I can help them with anything they need. Which is why I'm in a bakery helping my mom at 3am.

"What do you need me to do today?"

"Have you submitted any job applications?" she answers,

narrowing her brown eyes that are so much like mine. "I heard they are hiring in the factory."

It's too early to discuss money. I was hoping she would ask me to visit Dad in Portland, or maybe even stay here while she goes to visit. I shouldn't be surprised she needs money more than free labor. I had to buy some of the bakery supplies with my credit card last night.

"I applied for several jobs last night." I say, trying to ease her mind. "I'm trying to apply for positions that relate to what I was doing before."

"You could stay in town," she suggests, again.

How do I explain to her that there's nothing in here for me? Is she still hoping that one day I'll take over The Cookie Jar? She loves baking. That's not for me.

I shake my head. "Mom. I love you and I'm going to figure out a way to get you guys out of this financial mess. You won't have to sell the bakery." I don't mention that I don't plan to stay. I don't think she wants to hear that today.

She sighs. "I could use some help at the bakery." Her tone clearly says *I'm not upset, just disappointed*, and I can feel my younger self shudder.

This is going to be a long, yet, short day. Mom always sells out by two or three o'clock. I bet that today she'll sell out before noon. Everyone in town is going to make sure they drop by to see if it's true that Hadley is back in town. I don't mind seeing old faces. Even when I'm a grown woman, I'm still scared of gossip. The cruel and false words that are spread like wildfire. The spark falls into a branch and the forest burns down.

Of course, all they care about is the gossip. They're going to ask about my upcoming wedding with a certain Coloradan-businessman. They'll be checking for my ring or asking if my soon-to-be husband is with me. And because I have a mother that loves to tweak the truth, I'll have to find a way to avoid the conversation of how we're not together, and he's not rich, and *god*, small towns really are hell.

Not to mention, because I was living with him and working for him, I am now homeless, jobless, and penniless. If there's a lesson to learn from my tale it's that I have to be more assertive and practice my independence. For such an independent person, I depended a lot on him. To add insult to injury, our friends chose him. Even the cat chose to stay with the asshole. Mom only knows half of what happened. I'm not ready to hear yet another lecture from her.

At least I'll be fine while the people in this town dissect my life. I'm not the same introverted girl who left ten years ago.

"Sure, let's go to the bakery. I miss baking cookies," I say. If worse comes to worst, there's always the back of the store where I can bake and avoid the people.

Being strong, outgoing, and different doesn't mean I'm ready to deal with them.

BAKING IS an art that requires passion and dedication. Mom loves this bakery as much as she loves Dad and me. She spends hours baking everything that she needs for the morning rush. Only hiring a cashier or two to help so she can be in the kitchen most of the day.

Every generation our roles change. My grandmother liked baking enough, but the woman was savvy when it came to business. She hired a couple of bakers and partnered with a few hotels in Portland to provide them baked goods. When Mom took over, things changed and she stuck to baking the best pastries on this side of the Mississippi. She hired employees to help her with the business side of her craft.

"I thought you had people helping you," I say, confused as I stare at the fancy freezer on the storefront that says, 'Aldry's Sweets'.

In addition to the freezer, I can see shelves full of chocolates and candy, all labeled Aldry's Sweets. Since when did we start selling their products?

"We did," she confirms as she explains to me how to use the new register and the scanner that is used for the Aldry's products.

"What happened to your employees?"

"I had to let them go. I couldn't afford them anymore."

No wonder she was exhausted yesterday. She's already doing everything and she's planning to take care of Dad when he comes back home because we can't afford a nurse. There's no way she can keep doing this with no employees. We don't even have our goats anymore; she sold them to the Aldridges last weekend.

"Mom, how bad are the finances?"

"Not great," she answers before turning around and walking back to the kitchen. I follow right behind. "We still need to finish a few more batches of croissants."

She starts pouring the ingredients into the industrial mixer and I know the conversation is over. I go back to my station and roll the croissants carefully. If I manhandle the dough, they won't be as soft and crispy as Mom likes them. As I work, I can't help but wish she had told me before I left my job and left Randall. I could've lent her some money. Now we're both broke and desperate.

We focus on baking. There's no time for us to discuss Dad's current situation, the bakery, or my plans.

Do I even have plans?

I plan to leave this town. Right after I get a job that pays well enough so I can help Mom pay for whatever she needs. Whatever that may be.

I need more information about my parents' finances. They were doing fine, weren't they? She told me Dad was making money from his goat hobby. Did she lie to me? Is the bakery at risk? Is the house?

Thoughts about my parents' future are not only worrying me but giving me major anxiety. How am I supposed to help them? There has to be a solution. I do my best to clean the kitchen, bake more batches of muffins and croissants, and even bake the cookies for the ten o'clock rush.

It's around eight when Mom comes into the kitchen holding a white box and says, "Here, take this to the Aldridge mansion."

I want to ask why but I refrain. I can tell by her face that she's over today. There's no point in asking why they're too good to come to the store.

"As soon as I'm back, you're going to take a break, okay?"

Mom shrugs.

I rush through Main Street, wishing I could stop by A Likely Story Bookstore to say hello to my great aunt and buy a few books to read while I'm in town. The outside of the window shops are almost the same as they were while I was growing up. The buildings are a mix of Old West and Victorian eras, and at the end of it all is the Aldridge mansion.

The fence that surrounds it is made out of limestone. It's easy to climb and not too tall. I'd know, as I used to sneak in when the old Aldridge lady was still alive. The far east side of the house has a big rock next to a tree that is perfect for sitting and reading a book on a hot summer day. I used it often when the park was too busy.

The outside hasn't changed much, except for all the ways that it has. The old black iron gate has been restored or replaced with a newer replica. It's strange to find it closed. After old Lady Aldridge died, it was always open. That's when I used to come by to use the lake as my private pool.

There's something in front of the gate, reminiscent of a drive-thru dashboard. I press what I assume is the doorbell.

"How can I help you?" A husky voice answers.

I hold up the box. "I have a delivery from My Cookie Jar."

"Where is Paige?" the voice asks.

Busy, and I don't have time to explain myself.

"Can you just come outside to pick up the box?"

"Who are you?" The man's voice has a hint of annoyance.

"My name is Hadley," I say with a groan.

"Anyone know a Hayley?"

"Hadley!"

"Henry, open the door. I don't care if she's a Russian spy. She has my croissants," a woman snaps at the man.

"Fine," the man sighs. "You can come inside."

Why can't he come outside?

The gate opens. I walk toward the main house, but I can't help but stare at the charred building across from it. I guess that's the studio that exploded. If the house was in the same condition as when I was younger, it would certainly add more personality to its previously gothic style

It's a miracle that none of the trees burnt with the explosion. Maybe because it was built closer to the lake and further from the evergreens?

When I arrive at the main house, there's a pregnant lady by the door flanked by two tall men. She is smiling at me, her hair in dark waves resting on her shoulders. "You must be Hadley. I'm Sophia Aragon-Aldridge."

I present the box. "Did the goodies give me away?"

She shakes her head. "Your mom talks a lot about you and showed us your picture once," she states.

My stomach drops. What did Mom share with her? It's unnerving to stand here not knowing if I'm going to say something that'll contradict her.

"Hello," I say, handing it over.

She takes the box with both hands and hugs it. "You're a lifesaver. Henry and Pierce tried to go for our daily order but they said the store was swamped," she says, name dropping two of the Aldridge brothers.

"It was like the grand opening of *Melting Memories A la Mode*," one of the guys who is standing close to her complains. He's almost a foot taller than me and I notice how green his eyes are as he studies me. "You couldn't get near that place."

"It was worth waiting for a double fudge vanilla sundae," I say, remembering the grand opening. "A friend and I called in sick."

"You live in Denver?" he asks.

"Up until yesterday morning," I confirm.

"She is the social media director for the Denver Troopers," Sophia announces then points at the man who mentioned MMAM. "That's Pierce, and the one behind him is my husband, Henry."

They look a lot alike—both have the same green eyes. Pierce is slightly taller than his brother and his shoulders broader, but they're definitely brothers.

"Nice to meet you," I say, wondering what else Mom told her about me. There's one thing I'm sure she hasn't said just yet, so I do it. "I *was* the social media director."

Sophia arches an eyebrow, then leans in with a conspiratorial whisper. "Does that have to do anything with the inappropriate pictures that were posted online?"

"Maybe?" I answer and I can't help but grin.

I shouldn't because I might be in trouble for doing that, but a little vengeance on your cheating boyfriend just tastes too good not to.

"Do you know who posted them?" she asks in the same tone. "That person might get a gold medal or be blacklisted."

"I don't want to think what's going to happen to me, yet," I sigh, hoping that the Quintons forget about it and me.

Her eyes open wide as she gasps. "Why?"

"Randall, the general manager of the team, was my live-in boyfriend up until that day," I say, unsure why I'm telling her this. I haven't even told Mom yet. "Never mind."

"You were nice," she says and points at Henry. "I catch him cheating and I'm going all Lorena Bobbitt on him."

I frown, confused. "Who is Lorena Bobbitt?" Henry and I ask at the same time.

"She's famous for cutting her husband's manhood," Pierce explains while covering his crotch. "I followed that trial closely. If you need a lawyer, I'm your guy."

"I'd never cheat on you, babe. I love you," Henry says.

Sophia laughs and gives me a playful glance. "I love to keep him on his toes. The Bobbitt case happened too long ago. I just know it because Mom threatened Dad a few times with that while I was growing up. I'm sorry he cheated on you. You guys were engaged, right?"

Oh, my mother and her fact tweaking. Before I can say anything a kid's voice yells, "Mama?"

I frown but before I can reply, I have a pair of small arms wrapped around my legs. I look down and it's a cute toddler with blond hair wearing footie pajamas.

"Arden, sweetheart," Sophia says. "She's Hadley."

"Howdy!" He says, releasing my legs and looking up to me, and grinning.

He's the same boy from last night. I'm even more curious about him and his father.

Who is his father? He's one of the Aldridge brothers? Was that Mills? Everyone who follows hockey knows about him and his son. This sweet little boy might be him. I love kids. I've always loved kids. In all my time of loving kids, I have never, not once, wanted to have them. This kid makes me want to change my mind. The house, the people, and this adorable toddler are calling me in. I want to stay and get to know this little boy, maybe his dad, and everyone else.

I decide to chalk it up to curiosity, nothing more. Besides, it's time for me to leave. Mom is waiting for me.

"It was nice meeting everyone."

Chapter Seven

Mills

AN AVERAGE HOCKEY player gets around 22-24 minutes per game. Hockey players retire between the ages of thirty-three and thirty-seven according to a website. It really depends on many factors. I don't think there's an average. Most of the players retire because of an injury. After my last injury, the Vancouver Orcas released me from my contract.

Am I retiring?

Some days I'm hopeful that my knee is almost 100% recovered

because I might be able to play again. Others, it gives me anxiety just thinking that I'll never play again.

Overall, I can't foresee my future.

If I could, maybe I would have foreseen the call from Jean-Paul, my former agent, asking how I'm doing.

He wasn't wondering about my well-being but about my knee and the future of my career. He was wondering if I'm going to be able to play again.

I don't have an answer for him. It's not that I can't skate. Hayes, my older brother and one of the best orthopedic surgeons in the world, has been treating my knee. He brought the best physical therapists he knows. Hayes says it's good as new. We even went to Portland to try the ice rink, and I could skate without having any pain.

However, he warned me, "If you get injured again, you'll need surgery, and I won't clear you to play—ever again."

Do I want to go back and risk another injury?

That's debatable.

My house arrest—or what the lawyer likes to call the will stipulation—lasts until the end of November. That gives me plenty of time to think about the future and what I might want to do next year.

Am I ready to pack my things and leave?

It depends on the day. There are times when all I want is to fasten Arden in his car seat and drive away. Other times I'm so comfortable with my family that I consider the possibility of staying.

It helps that the house is flooded with dopamine. You know, that chemical substance that makes you behave like a complete fool because you're in love?

Four of my brothers are thoroughly whipped by their women. I never thought I'd say this, but those assholes make me feel lonely. As if there's a part of me that's been missing, one I didn't care about before. Now I have this internal—*irrational*— urge to find it, even if I don't need to be in a relationship.

Maybe it's because I haven't had sex since I found out about Arden. Seriously, I've been celibate for about three years. That's the only way to explain the weird attraction to Hadley, since all she did was sit by me on a bench last night. I must be fucking horny.

So while my mind and my life are packed with a gazillion issues, my agent only cares about one thing: am I going to play next season?

When I told him that I couldn't make any decisions until November, he politely excused himself and ended the conversation.

Thank you, useless friend.

I know he's not a friend. The guy sees me as a dollar sign. He doesn't care if my son is having trouble falling asleep. Or that my best friend, who is my youngest brother, is in the hospital fighting for his life.

Today would've been a great day to drive to Portland and spend the day with Arden. Instead, I spent all morning at The Lodge dealing with a long line of tourists who, aside from needing to check in, also asked for my autograph and a picture.

Listen, I love my fans, but it's hard to do the public figure gig while working. I can't just say, "I'm sorry, but I have to work." I should start messing up at the front desk just the way Beacon did. Maybe Henry will send me to the kitchen immediately.

It's around ten when Arden finally falls asleep. I'm mentally tired, but my body is restless. I change into a pair of sweats. As I make my way to the door, I hand the baby monitor to Sophia and Henry, who are in the living room.

"Where are you going this late?" Henry asks.

"I need to go for a run," I mumble.

"To the gym?"

"No, around town. Is that okay, Dad?"

"I won't apologize for being cautious. Should I remind you that only a month ago, the studio exploded, Beacon almost died, and several men were trying to kill us?" His voice comes out forcefully.

Under different circumstances, I'd tell him to fuck off, but I try to remember that he's dealing with what happened just a month ago, just like the rest of us.

"I'll be fine," I assure him. "I just need some fresh air."

If the ice rink was ready, I'd be burning some energy there. I can't wait until Easton's crew finishes it.

I run around town and stop right by the park to find the same woman from last night, sitting on the bench. My mind says it's time to head back home. My legs carry me all the way to where she is. There's something about her that feels familiar and comfortable.

Last night when I watched her with Arden, she scared me shitless.

She's practically a foot shorter than me, but her voice, her smile, and those big brown eyes are larger than life.

Is she pretty?

She's cute—lovely.

The woman has that girl next door vibe, like early 90's Jennifer Aniston, just starting on *Friends,* except Hadley's hair is wavy, and her body is curvier. Okay, I might've looked more closely than I want to admit.

One thing I know is that I don't need someone like her in my life.

So why am I here, standing in front of her, wondering where she came from and what she's doing in the park this time of night?

Those are too many questions from a guy who doesn't give a fuck. I shouldn't care that her face doesn't have the brightness that it had last night, or that her lips quiver as she focuses on the screen of her phone.

"Is everything okay?" I ask, stopping a few feet away from her.

She shakes her head, waving her phone. "If there's a lesson we should all learn from the mess I made, it should be, think before you post."

"Posting what?"

"On social media," she responds, still not looking at me.

Well, no one should be posting online. Mom says social media is the devil. It sounds like an exaggeration, but sometimes it's so true. "Wise words. I'm guessing you're talking from experience?"

She sighs and nods.

"Isn't it a little late to be out here in the park?"

She looks up at me. Her big expressive eyes carry a hint of worry. Maybe it's sadness. "It's better than laying on my childhood bed while I think about my parents' life. Mom might lose her shop. Dad's in the hospital. The insurance doesn't cover the specialists that he needs to recover. I can't find a job, and my ex just threatened to sue me because…" she pauses. "Because he's a cheating asshole."

My life doesn't sound so shitty compared to her current situation, and yet, I remember the way her lips turn upward and how her face brightens. As if she's competing with the moon's light. Her presence is brighter than the satellite. She makes her own sunshine. I hate that there's something dimming her light.

"There's a lot happening in your life."

She shrugs one shoulder. "It's life. How about you? Is Arden okay?"

I nod a couple of times.

A mischievous grin appears in her pouty lips. I'm curious to taste her heart-shaped lips. "I'm guessing you're Mills," she states.

"What gave it away?"

"I could lie and say it's a lucky guess. Add something crazy like you look like a hockey player—which you do. However, it's my job to know who you are. I just didn't recognize you last night," she answers, and before I can ask what that means, she explains herself. "I used to be the Social Media Director for the Troopers. I know you were the assistant captain and star defenseman of the Vancouver Orcas."

"That'd be me," I confirm.

"So far, I've met the CEO, the lawyer, and you," she states. "Three more, and I finish the quest."

"We are people, you know. This town makes us sound like a bunch of action figures. The lawyer, the doctor, the business guy, the musician, the dead one, the military guy, and the hockey player. We're not Ken dolls."

She laughs at my joke and I glare at her, pretending to be offended.

"Sorry, I get your point, but I was picturing..." she stops. "Never mind. I know it's hard to be the talk of the town. At least I'm taking the spotlight away from you."

I arch an eyebrow. "What does that mean?"

"I assume you haven't seen today's posts." She taps her phone and then hands it to me. "There's a poll. The town is wondering why I'm back without my big engagement ring. Am I pregnant with another guy's baby? Did he leave me at the altar? So far the first one is winning."

I check the phone to see Hadley, the baker's daughter, is back. There's even an option that says she's here for her Dad's funeral.

Rick Heywood died? I know he was in a car accident a couple of weeks ago. Vance airlifted him to Portland but he's not dead, is he?

"What happened to your dad?"

"He was in a car accident. They flew him to Portland," she answers, confirming my suspicions. "Mom didn't tell me how bad it was until I arrived in town."

"You're Rick and Paige's daughter?"

"They used to call me the baker's daughter," she answers with a sigh. "You get used to being called by a certain descriptor and never your name. If I were an action figure, I'd come with a fluffy white hat and an apron."

She might be from Baker's Creek, but she sounds like an outsider. I recall Paige talking about her. "Your mom told me once you work *in hockey*," I say, holding the laughter. I care about Paige but the way she says things is funny. "SMD for the team makes more sense."

"Is that what Mom told you about me?"

"A couple of times," I try not to laugh. "Her exact words were 'my Hadley works in hockey too.'"

"YEAH, but I got nothing on Mills 'Mean' Aldridge," she says, eyes narrowed

"I dropped the 'Mean' while I'm off the rink, but yes, that's me." I take a seat. next to her. "So, I take it you posted pictures for the team's social media?"

There are some pictures circulating far and wide that were originally posted on The Trooper's social media. They've made its way to my chats. I've got to admit, the pictures of the general manager fucking his girlfriend are funny. The video on YouTube is priceless. Mostly the voice of the woman who caught it all on camera, she was hilarious.

"So, did the account get hacked, or how did that picture of the GM get into the social media story?"

SHE STARES at the slide for a couple of beats before answering, "It's confidential
    information."

"WHICH IS WHY YOU GOT FIRED?"

"Nuh-uh. I quit and broke up with him after I found him doing his ex-wife in his office. The cheating asshole didn't lock the door. You could call me 'the scorned girlfriend.' Now I'm homeless, jobless, and penniless—and about to get served with a lawsuit for posting that picture."

I'd be suing her ass, too, if she posted a picture of me naked.

However, I wouldn't cheat on her to begin with. Not because I know she'd be bashing me online, but because no one deserves to be cheated on.

"So you're currently down on your luck, huh?" I try to cheer her up, but I don't know what else to say. She got herself into that conundrum.

"You've no idea."

I have a theory, which is that women don't think much when they're dating a wealthy man. They see a dollar sign and ignore the problems that go with it. I hate to think this woman is a gold digger, but why go out with an asshole like Quinton?

"Who dates a GM of a team? Or any rich bastard?" I say that out loud and regret it right away.

She huffs. "If I tell you that I thought he was the mailroom clerk, would you believe it?"

I shake my head.

"I'm what you might call "distracted." Also, I'm terrible at remembering faces and names."

"That's impossible."

"Not for me," she insists.

I cross my arms, frustrated by her lame excuse.

"While I can recite to you the periodic table of elements, I can't remember names and faces," she states. "It's why I told you I should know who you are. I would study hockey teams, players, statistics, and faces like studying for a standardized test. It'll be embarrassing to come face to face with Brock Dumas and not know that he's the captain of the Vancouver Orcas."

"You'd bruise his ego," I say, joking. Brock wouldn't give a shit. That guy is really down to Earth. I don't say that, though. "So you confused Quinton with the mailroom clerk?"

"Yep. We dated. He was nice, just like the three-year relationship we had—until he fucked up."

She doesn't sound like a woman in pain. "It sounds like you're over him."

"For the last couple of weeks, I've been analyzing the last three years of my life. I think this wasn't the first time he cheated on me. Also, there's no lost love. The last six months, he was absent. He wasn't the love of my life, but it was nice to date a grown man and have a steady relationship."

"A guy with money?"

"I didn't care about it. It was nice to live in a luxury apartment." She lowers her voice. "Which he didn't pay for. I paid half of it and the other half was covered by his parents."

"Not him?"

"Nope. If it wasn't for his family, he wouldn't have a penny. I contributed to the house," she says, almost offended.

Her phone buzzes. She closes her eyes and takes a deep breath. Then, placing that lovely smile on her lips, she says, "It's almost midnight, and you're listening to the loser of Baker's Creek blab."

"You shouldn't call yourself a loser."

"Oh," she chuckles. "That's how my classmates referred to me back in high school. Another reason why being here is like…hell or some kind of punishment. Tomorrow they'll line up at the bakery to get a peek of me. But I'll be baking while praying that someone calls me with a job offer."

"There are plenty of jobs in the factory," I offer.

"Will they pay enough to help Mom with the bakery before she loses it, recover Dad's goats, and pay his medical bills?"

I shrug because I have no idea how much money she needs to accomplish all of that, or if we even have a position at the factory to offer her.

"Selling one kidney might get the goats back," she chuckles, shoving her phone inside her purse and standing up. "Thank you for the company. Maybe next time, we'll talk about what's keeping you up all night."

I rise from my seat and begin to follow her. She glances over her shoulder and continues walking. "I don't need company."

"It's too late."

"It's Baker's Creek," she retorts.

"Humor me, okay?"

When we arrive at her doorstep, she looks at me and says, "You Aldridges are a lot different than I thought."

I'm not sure why I bend and kiss her cheek. The light of the moon allows me to see her cheeks turn slightly dark. She sucks her bottom lip nervously. I like that I have some effect on her and this attraction isn't one sided.

"Stick around, and you'll find out that we can be cool. Sleep tight, Hadley."

Chapter Eight

Mills

I WAKE up in the morning with more energy than I've had in a long time. I slept better than I have in several weeks, and Arden is still asleep. It gives me plenty of time to go to the gym and get ready to work before I have to wake him up. I tiptoe inside his room.

I squat and whisper, "Good morning, sport."

His eyes flutter open and his smile appears immediately. "Dada!"

I pick him up from his toddler bed. "Let's wash your face and have some breakfast."

When we reach the kitchen, I find Leyla roaming around. She's busy washing last night's baby bottles.

"Morning, Red," I joke, knowing she hates that nickname.

"Someone woke up with a death wish," she responds, turns around, and smiles at Arden. "How's my sweet boy?"

"Li-la," he says excitedly, opening his arms and pushing himself forward.

Leyla dries her hands with a hand towel and takes him into her arms. She hugs him tightly and spins him a couple of times. "I was wondering if you're free for a playdate later today. It's going to be just you and me. Well, and the goats."

At the mention of the goats, I recall Hadley. "So, why do we own goats?"

"Paige needed to sell them," she answers. "I offered to buy them since she wouldn't accept any financial help. Her husband lost his job at the high school last year. After his accident, there's no way they can keep them."

"Why are we whispering?" I match her tone of voice.

"Sorry, sometimes I feel like I'm in the middle of Main Street and someone might listen. Paige told me that in confidence. They pretended it was an early retirement. He was doing well with the goat-milk products, but he got into an accident. He won't be able to take care of the girls for a long time. Paige can't take care of them. She wasn't sure if her daughter was going to come and help them."

That's not what Hadley told me. Maybe she doesn't know about her dad's job.

"How much money do they owe in medical bills and loans?"

She narrows her gaze and studies me. "Why do you want to know?"

"Well, I was trying to understand why we have goats. You're telling me that Paige and the bakery are in trouble, I'd hate it if she had to close the place," I state, using my hockey-honed skill of dodging questions.

Reporters ask some dumb questions that are better answered by giving them the runaround. It's an art where you mix lies with diversion.

She gasps. "I didn't think that far. We should check with Hayes."

"What are you checking with me?" My brother asks as he enters the kitchen with Machlan.

I take the little boy from his arm. "Hey, dude. I heard you're working hard to take Carter's place as the loudest Aldridge in the family."

Hayes glares at me. "You're joking, but it's true. I swear it's the name, Carter. Carters are as loud and noisy. The two babies are taking after our brother Carter. From this point forward, no one is allowed to use that name again," he threatens.

I pat his shoulder. "We're in a good mood today."

He gives me the finger before turning his attention to Leyla. "What do you need to ask me?"

"Rick Heywood," she answers. "How is he doing? Are they able to pay his medical bills? Paige sold the goats. What's next, the bakery?"

He shakes his head. "I haven't looked into it. Paige came to see me yesterday, but I was too busy and tired to pay attention to her. She mentioned something about moving him to my small practice because maybe it'd be cheaper. I heard her daughter is back in town. She's either going to take charge of the bakery or take care of her dad."

"Why don't you call the hospital?" I suggest. "We could figure out a way to help them."

He glances at me. "Why?"

"Isn't that what we do? We help the town."

They aren't ready for the truth. I'm not prepared to discuss Hadley. In all my life, I've never had a female friend. It would be a little weird to say, "Well, I randomly met this woman in the park who I think I'm becoming friends with, and I'd like to help her."

Leyla and Hayes each give me a suspicious look, then look at each other.

"Why would I have an ulterior motive?" I ask.

"You usually open your wallet and say, 'Sure, just do whatever you want,'" Hayes answers. "You're never actively offering to help others. It's uncharacteristic of you."

"Paige adores Arden. I feel like she's done a lot for the family. We should be giving her a hand, don't you think?"

He nods. "I'll call today to figure out his situation."

"Their insurance might not pay for the therapies and aids they need to help him recover," I add, trying to remember my conversation with Hadley. If I can help her with at least one thing, she might be able to relax a little.

"What am I missing, Mills?" Hayes asks, tapping his chin with his index finger.

"Some sleep," I say, dodging his question. "Everyone is missing sleep in this house. I can't wait for the twins to be born. This house is going to become a war zone."

"You're probably right," he agrees.

I look at Machlan with a little guilt. With all the lies my brothers and I have been feeding Hayes our whole lives, there's no way he'll ever be able to get away with anything.

I CAN'T EXPLAIN why I'm at the park again, sitting on the bench where I found Hadley last night. It might be because of my early conversation with Paige, her mom. After work, I visited the bakery. One part of me wanted to see Hadley and another wanted to find out more about Heywood's situation. Paige was about to close the bakery when I opened the door and I think the only reason she didn't kick me out is because I have Arden with me.

"It's so nice to see you," she said. I'm unsure if she was talking to me or Arden. Probably Arden, she adores him.

"He had a great day and asked for cookies," I say, using my son as an excuse.

"I'm so sorry Hadley isn't here for me to introduce the two of you. She is great with kids. Have I told you that people used to book her services weeks in advance? The parents loved her almost as much as the kids. She is in Portland with Rick, but if you come by tomorrow, you might be able to meet her."

I answered politely that we would swing by soon.

It was my intention to see Hadley when we visited the bakery. Since I'm not waiting until tomorrow, well, I'm here at the park hoping that she'll show up. I'm still thinking about my earlier conversation with Paige.

What else was there to say? Was she suggesting that we hire her as a nanny? I'd love to offer Hadley the job—after running a background check on her—but we can't. According to the will's stipulations, we can ask a friend to help us take care of our kids, but we can't pay for the services because they fall into housework. Or was it housekeeping?

Whatever. There has to be another way to help her.

Why do I want to help Hadley? I don't even know. It's not like she's a friend or a family member; she's a woman I met two nights ago on a park bench. Do I find her attractive? Yes. There's no ulterior motive behind this wish to make things better—other than she's hot.

This is insane. I should go back home. I place my palms on my thighs getting ready to stand up when I hear her voice.

"I should charge you for using my bench."

When I turn around, I see her approaching me, her hair pulled up into a ponytail. She wears a pink sweatshirt and a pair of jeans.

"It doesn't say Hadley's property. We're becoming friends," I pause. "You should let me borrow it."

"It does," she answers.

"Is that so?"

She nods a couple of times. "Well, it would if whoever renovated the place hadn't sanded it and restored it." She jabs a finger pointing at me. "Plus, you were rude the night we met. I'm still not sure if I like you."

"I'm sorry for my behavior." She's right, I wasn't pleasant. It was a combination of lack of sleep, my entire family almost dying, and my son running toward a stranger. Since I don't want to burst her bubble by telling her that we changed all the equipment and this bench is brand new, I ask, "How's your dad?"

Taking a seat, she pulls out her phone and shows me a picture of a man in his forties with a little girl wearing pigtails. "Not like this. He's battered up, depressed, and anxious. Mom never told me they fired him. Well, they didn't renew his contract. He has been out of the job for almost a year. I don't understand why Mom didn't tell me. Their insurance is a joke. They are only covering twenty-five percent of the medical bills. He's been in the hospital for two weeks."

She breathes a couple of times. The two lines between her brows smooth out. She looks at her hands, then at me. "I have a plan. If I take a few graveyard shifts at The Lodge and work at the factory during the day, I might be able to finish paying by the time I turn fifty."

"What's going to happen to your career?"

"I killed it when I posted that stupid picture of my ex-boyfriend." She sighs long and loud. "It's not like my career matters. They need me. This is what you do when your family needs you. You pull yourself together and do the best you can to keep them afloat. They'd do the same for me. We're The Three Musketeers."

That's a foreign concept to me. When I was growing up, if I needed my father, he'd ignore me. When my brother Carter got sick, he didn't even reach out to us, knowing that the Aldridges' motto is: *you're on your fucking own*. We're no musketeers.

"I'm going back tomorrow to pick him up," she continues. "I spoke to his doctor who said it's okay to take him with me. I talked to the contractor earlier today to see if he could help me modify the house. After he gave me the quote, I almost offered to pay him with a kidney because I don't have that kind of money. I could go to Happy Springs and audition at the strip club."

As hot as it'd be to watch her strip, I'm sure we can find a better solution. "What can I do for you?"

"Sorry, I'm taking up your time. Tonight we're supposed to talk about you." She changes the subject. "Tell Hadley what's keeping you up."

Just like that, the conversation is closed, and her face is sporting a smile. Surprisingly, it doesn't seem fake. She's genuinely happy. How can she be? She reminds me of Paige, who always has nice words and a big smile for all her customers. It upsets me that she does so much for the town, and the town isn't doing shit for her or her family.

"Is it your career? Are you retiring?" she questions.

I'm guessing she wants to forget about her problems for now. "Off the record?" I say, giving in.

She chuckles. "I'm not a reporter. It's not like I'm going to sell the story. Hockey fans adore learning about you guys, but it's not like celebrities. The stories don't sell well. Now, if it was your brother Beacon."

"He's not up for discussion," I say firmly, stopping her before she tries to get any information about him.

"I'm not discussing him. What I was going to say is that anything about him would sell. He's the guy you would want to protect." She sighs. "I'm desperate but not an asshole."

I could tell her that I'm protective of Beac. Instead, I say, "I'm not sure what's going to happen next year. I love playing, but I can't take another hit on my knee."

"Can you bubble wrap it before every game?" she grins, shaking her head. "It's okay to want to do other things. The average person changes careers every ten to fifteen years."

My heart skips a fucking beat. My heart never does that. Did she just quote averages? A woman after my own heart. And maybe this is why I came to the park. It's so easy to talk to her, it feels like we're on the same frequency.

"What do you think I should do if I retire?"

She gives me a once-over with her eyes. "You could become a model."

"So people can ogle at me?"

"I would buy a few pictures of you, blow them up and cover my walls with them."

I snort. That's ludicrous. "Posing for pictures sounds painful. Any other options?"

"You can be an actor," she continues. "Use those good looks. The only professional hazard would be kissing actresses on command."

She barks out a laugh.

"Why is that funny?"

"It's just funny," she says teasingly, as if she holds onto a special secret. She drags her tongue across her bottom lip, grinning playfully. "Unless you don't know how to kiss."

That challenging smirk has a strange effect on me. My lips crave hers. I want a real taste of Hadley, want to kiss her like she's never been kissed.

"But I do," I say, threading my fingers through hers and bringing her hand to my lips. "Well, I used to know how to do it. It's been years. I would have to practice," I whisper as I softly place kisses along her knuckles.

That throaty noise coming from her pushes me to do something I haven't done in years.

I reach the back of her neck with my free hand, and I lean closer to her, close enough to feel her breath warming my skin.

"Can I show you?" I dare to ask because I don't want to just take it.

"Can I kiss you, Had?"

Her voice is a soft whisper. "Yes."

I brush my lips over hers. Once. Twice. Then, I dip my mouth to hers. Never in my life have I put any thought into a kiss. This time though, I don't want to mess it up. It's just as important as handling the stick just right as you're about to pass the puck. One wrong move and the perfect play might ruin your career.

In this case, it might end what could be a lifetime in heaven. I slide my tongue across her lips, and she opens them while she wraps her arms around my neck. I pace myself, enjoying each lazy swipe of our tongues, enjoying the feel of her body against my body, sucking down on those throaty moans that are quickly becoming my favorite sound.

I move my lips to her jawline, nibbling her soft skin all the way to her earlobe.

She tastes sweet. Like flowers, cookie dough, and sugar. I could devour her. Nibble every inch of her skin, drink her in.

I don't.

I stop myself before we do something we regret. We're in the park. I refuse to expose her and make her the talk of the town—more than she already is. I've heard enough people talking as it is.

"Sorry, I got carried away," I apologize, tracing her bottom lip with my thumb.

Her brown eyes stare at me with the same lust I feel. "That was…" she pauses. "Nice."

"Oh, no, baby. You don't call me nice."

I claim her mouth, this time deepening the kiss. This time I don't hold anything back, and neither does she. We're both desperate and hungry.

This time, she's the one who stops us. "I have to go home." She springs out of the bench and takes off.

I follow behind her. When she stops at her doorstep, she finally looks at me. "That shouldn't happen. I'm not in a good place."

"Sorry," I apologize. "If I promise to behave tomorrow, will you still be at the park?"

She nods.

Chapter Nine

Mills

TODAY IS one of those days when I'm thankful for Sophia's parents. They visit often, and when they're in town, they're the ones who help me with Arden. I spend my morning at the factory pretending to work but mostly thinking about Hadley.

Last night after kissing her, she was all I could think about. I spent an hour in the shower taking care of myself because every time I think of Hadley, her soft hair, her glowy skin, and those pouty lips, my cock gets hard as a rock.

My brothers should be thankful that I didn't have to work at

The Lodge, or I'd have upgraded everyone, offered some complimentary breakfast, or given a free night because I'm too fucking distracted.

When the workday is over, I drive home. I plan on walking to Aragon's place to pick him up. When I'm walking from the garage to the main house, I spot Emilio and Natalia Aragon in the outdoor arena with Leyla, Arden, and the horses. So much for having an excuse to drop by the bakery.

As I head toward the main house, I spot Sophia and Henry. They're sitting on the porch swing.

"Taking the afternoon off?" I joke.

"Fuck off," Henry growls, kissing his wife's belly. He shows me a book. "I'm reading to my kids."

I envy my brothers. That's something I didn't experience when Margaret was pregnant. The first kick, the heartbeat during the sonogram, anything that involves the development of a baby before they are born. Since I didn't agree to marry her, she refused to move to Vancouver. If I wanted to see her or learn anything about the baby, I had to travel to Indiana, which was almost impossible.

"I'm glad you're here," Sophia says, bringing my mind to a complete stop.

"I live here," I reply.

"We need to discuss childcare. Your suggestion to open one in Aldry's is good, but to build it will take some time. We can set up a nursery in one of the empty offices, but we still need help." She takes a deep breath. "My parents can't handle five children. They aren't that young anymore. Have you asked around?"

Hadley could be a great option, but I doubt she'll say yes to step in when we can't offer her any money. Plus, kissing would become impossible. I can't just make out with the nanny. How cliché is that?

"Mills, are you paying attention?" Sophia waves a hand in front of me. "You were distracted earlier, during our meeting. Now you are...what's happening to you?"

"Lack of sex," Henry jokes.

I glare at him. "Shut the fuck up, Henry."

He sets the book down and presses his hands on the sides of Sophia's belly. "Shh, don't curse in front of my children."

"You miss Beacon so much that you're trying to be the funny one?" I stare at Sophia, hoping she'll control her man.

"Speaking about Beac," he says. "Hayes was telling us that he should be here in a couple of weeks. His bandmates are coming with him. That'll be good because they can help with his recovery while we keep covering for him."

"Any chance that Grace can be our designated sitter?"

That was the original plan until Beacon got hurt. She spends all her time in the hospital taking care of him.

Sophia shakes her head. "I wouldn't count on her."

"Paige's daughter," I blurt the words without thinking.

Henry gives me a strange look. "What about her?"

"Paige always says that she was the babysitter of the town." I almost high-fived myself for thinking on my feet so fast.

"She's not seventeen anymore." Sophia rolls her eyes. We're exasperating as fuck. "She was a social media director. I might be able to get her something at Aldry's or at Markels if she needs a job. There are other places she can go where diaper changing or dealing with the Aldridge brothers won't be involved."

"It was an option," I offer. "Are you hungry? Maybe you're missing your late afternoon cookies, and that's why you're grumpy."

Sophia rubs her belly and moans. "You're right. The babies and I need cookies."

That sounds more like she needs sex, but I'm not saying a word about it. "You owe me," I tell Henry, pivoting toward the gate.

"I don't owe you shit," he yells. "You're willingly going for the cookies because you have a crush on the baker's daughter."

I flip him the finger and walk away.

"HELLO, MS. PAIGE," I greet her as I enter. I notice the display cases are empty. "You're ready to pack and leave?"

She nods. "Rick and Hadley should be home soon. Your brother, Vance, offered to fly her when the doctor heard Hadley was driving to pick him up."

She gives me a box of cookies. "Here. This is for you. I know this won't repay everything your family has done, but it's something."

"Is there anything else we can do, other than flying your husband?"

She shakes her head. "No. We'll be fine. Easton Rodin is at the house fixing it so my husband can get around."

I'm glad to hear that Easton did as I requested. Let's hope he keeps my secret too. I begged him not to tell anyone that I'm the one paying for his services and the material.

"If you need anything, just reach out to us," I offer.

"You remind me of your dad," she says.

Is she calling me a cold bloodsucking bastard?

"Hopefully not, ma'am. I've worked hard not to be like him." My voice has more anger than I intended.

"Not that William," she says. "He was different. He used to work for my mom. I had a little crush on him because he was really nice."

"My father?"

She nods. "I was seven. He always brought me a lollipop or a bar of chocolate from the factory."

"What happened to him?"

"It's hard to know," she responds. "Your grandmother wasn't a nice woman. I never met your grandfather, but no one has anything nice to say about him either. I guess they forced him to change. I just hope you guys don't end up like him."

"What do you mean?"

"None of you have anything nice to say about him. It doesn't require much to guess that you weren't close to him. It wasn't until he died that you finally came back to the town." She wipes her already clean counter and then smiles at me. "If you guys leave, I hope you come back—and that you won't screw up the town before you go."

I pull out a hundred-dollar bill and set it in the tip jar. "We wouldn't do that."

Not intentionally, anyway. There are still a few more months to go before we meet my father's stipulations. A lot of things can go wrong. What if we fail?

AFTER DINNER, my brothers and I gather around the fire pit. Arden is in the barn "helping" with the baby chicks, a.k.a. watching them while Leyla makes sure that they're okay. One of the goats got into their area and knocked over the chicken coop.

"How is Rick?" I ask Hayes casually.

He gives me a look. "Is there something you want to share with us?"

"I'm asking a question," I retort, playing dumb.

"Rick is fine," he answers, not moving his gaze from me.

"Good, I was just wondering since Paige mentioned earlier that Vance was giving him a ride home."

He nods slightly. "Do you happen to know who hired Easton?"

"Dude, we hire him for everything," I respond.

"Sure, but someone anonymously hired him to do a setup similar than the one we have for Beac here," he continues. "I'm just curious about this unknown benefactor."

I shrug.

"He has a thing for Paige," Henry suggests.

"His daughter is cute," Vance offers.

I shoot daggers at him.

Hayes shouts, "I fucking knew it. You have a thing for Hadley. You've been weird since she arrived."

All my brothers stare at me, judging. This is a make-or-break moment. I'm right in front of the goalie and if I shoot at a wrong angle, I'm screwed. The team loses and I'll go down as the idiot that fucked the entire season.

"We have rules. One that includes you can't go out with the townies. They are off-limits," Henry warns me. "If you fuck up things will get sticky."

"I don't have a thing for her. She's nice, like her mom. Do you know our father used to work at the bakery?"

Their attention shifts immediately to what I just said. My brothers are easily distracted. Give them some catnip about our father's past, and they get off your case immediately.

Chapter Ten

Mills

I DON'T REMEMBER who came up with the stupid rule about hooking up with people from Baker's Creek or Happy Springs. We just agreed that we wouldn't screw around. It makes sense. You don't want to be the womanizer of the Aldridges. That's not how I want to be known in this town.

Does that mean I should stop seeking out Hadley?

I'm not sure, and I don't fucking care.

Can we even consider Hadley a townie?

She left this place right after high school and doesn't seem to belong any more than we do. At the end of the day, I don't need excuses to see her. My brothers can go and fuck themselves. I am my own person. It's around ten when I decide to go on a run.

The shadow of Vance startles me. He's leaning against the wall.

"You're so fucking predictable," he grumbles.

"Are you my designated babysitter?"

He shakes his head a couple of times. "I'm here to warn you. You're playing with fire."

A wave of nausea hits me. Is there another threat? How many people want to kill him? I try to keep my cool and ask casually, "What are you talking about?"

"This will be the third night you meet with Hadley—without Arden," he states.

The knot on my stomach loosens up slightly, but now I'm fucking angry. "Have you been spying on me?"

He shakes his head. "There are eyes everywhere."

Who is watching us other than the nosy habitants of Baker's Creek? I recall having the high-intelligence security company that Beacon works for patrolling the town after we were attacked but —"Beacon's people?" I ask, scanning our property.

He nods.

I swallow hard, trying not to panic. "Why? I thought it was over."

"We just want to make sure it's safe," he responds.

"We? Are you working for them?" Vance is like a Rubik's Cube. You think you already have him figured out, but you've only solved one side of the puzzle. The other five are a mess.

"It doesn't matter," he mumbles. "The point is that you need to stay away from the baker's daughter. She's leaving soon, and you can't go after her."

That doesn't make sense. Why would I chase her? Does he think I'm going to fall in love with her? We're friends and...

"What if she stays?" I ask because I don't want her to leave just yet.

"That's even worse," he states. "You hookup, your son gets attached, and what's going to happen when you leave?"

For a pragmatic guy who doesn't give a shit about feelings, he sure is blowing things out of proportion.

"You have no idea what you're talking about, asshole. Hadley is a friend," I state. It may be a bit of an exaggeration considering we just met.

"I know exactly why I'm telling you to stop. After our father, Mom dated a really cool guy. He lived with us, and I even called him Dad. After they broke up, I never heard from him. Just think about it, I was abandoned by my father and then by this man. If you end up fucking her, keep your son away. Guard his heart, or he'll be fucked up before he turns five."

That would've screwed me up, too, not that I'm that sane. "You never told us about that."

While growing up, my mom married twice, but I always got along with her husband in turn. I still call them on their birthday and we even text every now and then. They do the same with me, never making me feel like I'm not a part of their life anymore. Maybe I was lucky, or Mom knew how to handle my relationship with her partner in turn. Who knows?

"It doesn't matter," he groans. "I'm just giving you some friendly advice."

I recall his mom is married. "What about your current stepfather?"

He snorts. "We don't get along. I don't know if it was because I rejected him or didn't care to bond with him. It might be a combination of everything. Mom always made sure I knew I wasn't part of her new family, even though I lived with them until I was eighteen."

See what I mean about this guy being complicated? I'm impressed that he's confiding in me. Our relationship can be summarized into a few texts and two phone calls for the past eight years.

"Listen, Hadley is just a friend. Her life is a clusterfuck. I know where Hadley and I stand, but thank you for worrying about Arden's wellbeing."

As I walk away, he says, "I'll beat the shit out of you if I see you or your kid broken-hearted."

I wave at him, not turning around. "Joy. Nothing says brotherly love better than threats of physical violence."

WHEN I ARRIVE at the bench, Hadley isn't there. I wait for an entire hour before I walk toward her parents' house. I just want to make sure that she's okay, since I know she just brought her father back from the hospital.

I'm about to cross the street when I see her walking toward me. When she spots me, the corners of her lips tilt toward the sky. There is something about that mouth, maybe her smile, that loosens everything inside me.

"Where are you going this late at night?" she asks as she reaches me.

"I wanted to check on you." I tilt my head toward the mansion. "Follow me."

"That's pretty sweet." She pauses. I don't turn to look at her because I want us to go to a safe place. If someone sees us talking, this town is going to blow our friendship out of proportion. "I met Military Ken and Doctor Ken."

"Seriously, Hadley?"

She makes some weird noises, and when I turn to look at her, I notice her shaking with laughter.

"Where are we going?" she asks as we pass the park.

"Trust me," I request, going toward the wooded area that's behind our property.

Thankfully, the code for the door that takes us to the underground apartment that Beacon owns still works. "Let's go."

"Are you kidnapping me?"

"No, I'm taking us to a place where no one can see us," I answer, turning the switch that brings all the lights to life.

"This didn't exist before," she mumbles as we make our way through the tunnel. "Why would you have a...Is this some kind of bomb shelter?"

"How do you know it wasn't here?"

"After your grandmother died, this became party central for some," she states. "For me, it was my private swimming pool."

"That explains why it was such a mess when we came back," I sigh, grabbing her hand as we continue our way through the long and creepy hallway. "So you threw big parties here, huh?"

"Not me," she assures me. "I'm the outcast of the town, remember?"

I stop, and when I turn to look at her, I understand why we pull toward each other like magnets. We're both alone in this forsaken town. My loneliness calls to hers. Sure, I have my brothers, but they are busy with their lives. The one person I'm close with is Beacon, and he's in the hospital. I know intimately how well she can relate.

Vance is slightly right. I shouldn't get close to her. What if she gets the wrong idea and she expects a lot more from me? All I want is someone I can talk with who understands me. It's rare to find someone who is so funny and easy to talk to. The kisses, though, they have to stop. *We* have to stop.

When we arrive at Beacon's place, she whistles. "Wow, this is better than the park or my bedroom. Not that I could invite you to hang out with me."

"This might be a late request because you're already here, but can you not tell anyone about this place?"

She snorts. "You're the only person I can talk to in this town. I love my mother dearly, but anything I tell her is used in the gossip mill."

"Thank you."

"So why are we here?"

I can't tell her that I just found out that my brother and the security agency are watching us. It sounds beyond weird.

"It's more private than the park. What if someone in town sees us and gets the wrong idea?" I respond.

"No one is out that late, but you're right. The people in this town can be a little extra." She grabs a small guitar. "Arden's?"

"Yes, my brother and his girlfriend entertain him with music," I say, sighing. I miss Beacon a lot.

"How is he doing?"

"Better," I answer, then look up at her. "Sorry, I was assuming—"

"You assumed right. I was asking about your brother. It sounds like he got hurt pretty bad. Was it the explosion?"

"No. It was during a concert." I stick to what his PR company published.

"We both know that's a lie, but if you want to stick with that…" she pauses. "I wouldn't tell anyone, but I understand why you're so reserved. It's hard to trust anyone."

"How is your dad?"

"Physically okay, emotionally he's a mess. He's the man of the house, and he's not only unemployed but also crippled." she pauses and winces. "Those are his words. I want to help him, but I don't know where to start. I feel like he was wrongfully terminated. Mom is trying to be strong for both of them, but she's struggling. She trusted that I'd be able to aid them. Instead, I'm here mooching off of them."

"Is there anything I can do for you?"

"You're already doing a lot. Not just anyone is willing to listen to my issues." She strums the guitar before giving me a look. "What's new with you? We're still trying to figure out what has you so restless."

Her brown eyes look at me intently.

"You know about my brother being in the hospital. I'm worried about him. With two babies and two more coming up, we're in urgent need of someone to help us take care of them," I state. "The only problem is that we can't hire anyone to help us with that."

"So you need someone to work for free?" She arches an eyebrow. "That's a tall order. I would say try the high schoolers, but even they need some form of payment. Why can't you hire a nanny?"

I wish I could confide in her but I can't. Even when I feel like I could trust her, I'm not there, and this isn't just about me but my family.

"It's complicated," I respond, stepping closer to her.

Her gaze darts from my eyes to my mouth. Her teeth scrape her bottom lip while she looks at me with uncertainty and desire. A desire I know so well because it's taking over my mind and my heart. I give in to the urge and bend, kissing her temple. "We can't talk about it but I can think of a few things I could do with you." I stroke my fingers along the edge of her jaw.

"Can you now?" Her voice is high, nervous. Her stunning big, brown eyes glint with happiness or maybe mischief.

Oh, she has no idea how much I could do—and how much I'd want to do to her. I lift her chin with my index finger, brushing my lips over hers before I feather her eyes and nose with kisses.

"We call this the game room. Would you like to play? I can think of a game or two. Like naked poker or—"

"It's strip poker," she interrupts me with a sultry voice that turns the heat inside me a few degrees more. "I don't think I'm ready to play that kind of game with you."

"How about if I just kiss you?" I whisper close to her lips I can feel her warm breath.

She nods once and I release her chin, slanting my mouth on hers. Hadley grabs the back of my head moaning into my mouth. I kiss her slowly, but possessively. Seduced by the possibilities I not only open my mouth as I deepen the kiss, but maybe my soul and probably my heart.

I tease her with my mouth as my hands slide up and down her curves. I don't know when she's leaving or if I'll have to stop seeing her. For now, I want to just hang on to her, learn more about who she is, and forget that I'm stagnant. At least until I can leave this town.

Chapter Eleven

Hadley

"WHERE WERE YOU LAST NIGHT?" Mom asks as I enter the kitchen.

I've been running from the bakery to the house all day long. Who needs a gym membership when you can just try to split yourself in half? This has been my life for the last week. At night, I get to spend time with Mills, but it's the first time she's mentioned my absence. I arrive home way past midnight because spending the night making out with Mills and learning trivial things like his love for facts and statistics is a lot better than sleep.

"Don't we have customers?" I ask, hoping that she'll go back to the front of the bakery and leave me to bake. It's one o'clock. If I make enough cookies, we might be able to stay open until four, and then we can sell more Aldry's ice cream and candies. I noticed yesterday that the middle and high school kids come after school and buy many of their products. We lose those sales the days Mom closes early from the lack of baked goods.

"I turned on the closed sign for a few minutes," she answers, crossing her arms and narrowing her eyes. "We need to talk. Where were you last night?"

"At the park," I lie smoothly.

If I tell her, 'I was hanging out with Mills at the Aldridges' secret bunker,' she's not going to be happy. Especially if I add in the part where we were making out on the couch. That's a fight we can't afford to have. I need a place to live and she needs someone to help her with Dad and the bakery.

That's not the only reason. If Mom finds out that I have any contact with the brothers, she'll use that morsel of information to drive more people into the store. I understand that she needs more sales, but I won't let her do it at their expense.

"You're not a teenager anymore," she says. "Do you know what can happen to you? It's dangerous."

Is she against me being outside the house after hours or hanging out with the Aldridges? When she talks about them, it sounds like she likes them well enough. Why is she all of a sudden saying you need to stay away from them? This town is a puzzle, more than a tourist destination.

"Mom, it's Baker's Creek," I remind her.

She gives me that look I hate so much, the one that tells me just how gullible and innocent she thinks I am. She opens her mouth, and is interrupted by a loud knock on the back door.

"Hadley Heywood? We're looking for Hadley Heywood."

Mom arches an eyebrow and sets her hands on her hips.

"I didn't do anything." I rush to defend myself before she begins to blame me for whatever is behind door number one. I don't know what's going on but it feels like trouble, and I'm sure whatever it is will unleash Mom's disapproval. She'll give me her passive-aggressive glare, the almost condescending and angry voice, and I'll be left feeling like the most stupid person in the world. I'll say stuff that she won't like, then I'll leave because I would rather sleep in my car than live with her silence.

"Stay here," she orders. "I'll go and see what's happening."

"Mom, I can take care of it," I argue, sauntering behind her.

When she opens the door, I see a man dressed in a cheap suit. I step next to Mom and I notice him holding a manila envelope.

"Hadley Heywood?" He looks at me, handing me the envelope. "You've been served."

Fuck!

"What is that?" Mom asks.

As I open it, my stomach drops. It's not one but two separate lawsuits. The team is suing me for misusing the social media account and damaging their reputation. Randall is suing me for using his and Suzie's picture without consent.

"My life is over," I mutter.

Placing the papers back into the envelope, I grab my phone and call my social media bestie. To avoid Mom eavesdropping on my call, I let myself inside the industrial fridge. Persy and I don't know each other that well, but we support each other a lot despite never having met in person. We send each other SEO tips and teach each other new tricks because the online business changes almost every day.

"Hadley!" She greets me. "How's it going?"

"Social media laws," I say, instead of answering her question. "Is there a lawyer for that?"

"Uh-oh, are those pictures coming back to fuck you in the ass?"

"Persy, Nova is right here," I hear another woman chiding her.

"Oops, sorry, let me take this outside," she mumbles. "Okay, what's happening?"

"They're suing me. I don't know who to contact or what to do,"

I answer, flustered as I pace back and forth inside the industrial fridge where I'm hiding from my mother.

God, what is my life?

"My sister is a lawyer, but she's on maternity leave. Her partner might be able to help."

"Are they expensive?"

"Do you need financial help?" she asks, and I want to say yes, but I can't repay anyone.

If I can get a hold of a lawyer, I might be able to convince them to work pro-bono or refer me to a cheaper option. No one is going to hire me after this, I certainly can't afford this nonsense.

"I'd like to avoid paying a lot," I respond. "I'm still in between jobs and helping my parents."

"You're pretty good at handling social media. Why don't you offer your services? I receive at least three messages a day asking if they could hire me for that work. I could refer them to you," she suggests. "You don't need to work for a big corporation to make a living."

"If they ask for my experience? I can't tell them who I used to work for or—"

"Listen, I would've done the same thing that you did," she says. I can hear the grin in her voice. "Maybe I would have used my own account, but I definitely would've posted that picture. You made that go viral within an hour. That's some powerful shit, and it shows how good you are at your job."

She's right. I don't need to disclose who I worked for in order to do any consulting jobs or handle a social media account. I just don't know if I have time to do it, and I need a computer to set up a website. Maybe I could use the bakery's laptop. This phone call might not have the answer to the lawsuit, but Persy has given me a seed of hope. It might be the answer to my long-term problems.

"If you could send them my way, I'd appreciate it."

"There's the kick-ass woman I know," she cheers. "Let me see if Nyx knows anyone."

"Thank you for being here for me."

"You're always here for me too," she answers. "If you need anything else, call me, okay?"

When I come out, Mom is leaning against the wall, arms crossed.

"What are you hiding from me?"

I show the papers to her. "I have a legal issue. You don't need to worry about it, though."

She shakes her head.

"Yes, I know you're disappointed. I'm twenty-nine, and I don't have my life together like the children of your so-called friends. They have sons-in-law, grandchildren, and stories that you can never match. Nothing has changed. I was never the cheerleader, the prom queen, or the popular one. This is what you got."

"Hadley."

I can't figure out her tone and I'm not sure that I want to. "I'll fix everything," I say, barreling over her. "In a few months, after Dad recovers, I'll leave. You'll be able to tell your friends that I'm with some rich asshole who you adore, that I live in a mansion, and if you're lucky, I'll give you a grandchild before I turn forty."

Before I can fix their financial issues, leave town, and start a new life, I have to fix my new problem. I lift the envelope, waving it at her. I'm ready to storm out of the bakery. I love my mom, but right now I don't like her. Maybe it's me who I don't like. Maybe I am disappointed in myself and reflecting those feelings on Mom. Perhaps we both feel the same, *we don't like Hadley at the moment.*

"I need to take this home. I'll be back in a few minutes."

AS I'M MAKING my way toward my house, I see Mills. He wears a dark suit and a grey tie that contrast with his green eyes, making him look even more handsome than he already is.

And there I go, lusting after the man. I've been trying to

convince myself that nothing is happening between us and the kisses we've shared... well they don't mean anything.

"You okay?" he asks.

I want to tell him no, ask him to hug me, to hold my hand, so I don't feel like drowning.

"I've had better days," I answer. My voice is cold, just like my hands.

He scans my face. "Anything I can do to help?"

I raise my hand waving the envelope with a defeated shrug. "If you know a cheap lawyer, maybe. If not..." I slump my shoulders. It takes me only a few seconds to realize there are people around watching us. "Sorry, I got to go. The bakery is still open."

I pass the bookstore. I wave at the ladies who are outside the door, but don't stop to chat with them. As I am about to turn on Mount Street, Mills catches up with me. "My brother's firm is the other way, and I was heading there to pick up Arden. Why don't you talk to him?"

I stop and turn to look at him. "Will he see me on such short notice?"

He takes the envelope. "We'll make it happen, follow me."

We speed walk toward our destination. Neither one of us speaks. My incoherent thoughts ramble about what can happen if I can't hire a lawyer. I wonder if this will send me to jail. My lungs stop pulling air for a second. I remember to breathe. I count the glass doors to each of the shops. The dry cleaner, the salon, the coffee shop. My heartbeat is almost normal. We arrive at a cute pink house that's across the street from the new animal clinic. He presses a code and opens the door. "Come inside. We can discuss what's happening here."

"Can you knock on the ducking door?" A guy who looks a lot like Mills if he had darker hair is glaring when we enter the room.

I arch a brow, almost laughing at the word. "Ducking?"

They both turn to look at me in unison. "Don't ask."

"Why are you here, and who is she?"

Mills hands him the manila envelope.

"Hadley Heywood," I say, jabbing my finger toward the envelope. "I'm here to see the lawyer."

He studies me for a couple of seconds without opening the envelope. His phone buzzes and he finally pulls his gaze from me to check it.

"If you'll excuse me, I need to take this call."

He goes inside his office and closes the door.

"What happened?" Mills asks.

"The team and my ex are suing me."

He shakes his head. "What do they want?"

"I didn't read them well. I just know that they are seeking damages for misusing the team's property."

"What does Quinton want?" he rephrases his question.

It's clear that he hates Randall. Do they have some kind of feud?

"Money, which he knows I don't have."

His jaw twitches. "Pierce will fix this."

Sure, he could probably fix it, but I still can't pay him. I try to think about what other vital organs I can sell without dying. Maybe a piece of my liver could pay the first lawsuit. I already promised my kidney to pay Dad's medical bills.

The time between Pierce taking the call and him coming out of his office feels eternal. I stand, nervously, wringing my hands. I wait for him to decline his help but instead he asks, "Do you know the Brassards?"

"I know Persy," I answer. "Well, we collaborate, but we haven't met. You know how it is, you contact someone online to ask questions about their Instagram, and the next thing you know, you're drinking virtual margaritas with them."

He gives me a puzzled look. "I wouldn't know. You talk a lot." He looks at his brother. "She talks a lot."

Mills nods once.

"So, do you know them?" The guy insists.

"I helped Persy Brassard set up one of her social media accounts when she was starting her blog." I roll my eyes. The answer won't change if he asks me the same question several times. "Since then, we've been helping each other."

"Well, her sister is my partner. She just called talking about a couple of lawsuits similar to what you just brought me."

"Can you help her?" Mills asks.

He nods and extends his hand. "Pierce Aldridge. We met the other day when you brought pastries to my sister-in-law, Ms. Hadley. I have to read both lawsuits before we can discuss your options. Can you come back tomorrow morning?"

I hate to answer no, but Mom needs me. "Could it be later? My mom needs help with the bakery and Dad needs me to watch after him. He can't walk."

He frowns. "Right, you're Rick and Paige's daughter."

"That'd be me."

He exchanges a look with Mills that ties the knot in my stomach tighter. Is this worse than I thought? Oh, God, I need a miracle. Just one, maybe a couple. Is this the part of the grieving process when I start bargaining? Not that I'm grieving but I do need to bargain with someone about the outcome of this mess.

"How about tomorrow around three? Can you make it work?"

"Yes." I shake his hand, hopeful that this is a step in the right direction. "Thank you."

"Don't thank me just yet."

The way he says it scares me. It suddenly becomes clear that if he can't help me, I'm going to end up in jail.

Chapter Twelve

Mills

"WHAT'S HER STORY?" Pierce asks after Hadley rushes out of the house. She has to bake cookies before her mom closes the bakery for the day.

"I think she has several stories."

If only he knew. The poor woman fucked with a brat and had to come home to find her parents in a rut. She's a little too cheerful to live in a fucked up world like this one.

Poor Hadley, running around with a little cloud above her head blocking the sun.

He arches an eyebrow. "How do you know her?"

"I met her at the park when I took Arden," I answer, hoping that he doesn't start interrogating me.

"Nyx gave me a little back story about this case. It's going to be a shit show. She mentioned that the woman doesn't have a job. You know she can't afford me, right? If I do this, she's going to be in debt with me for the next lifetime."

"Who owes you money?" Leyla, his wife, steps into the foyer. "Hey, Mills. Arden is napping along with Carter."

"No one owes me money yet. Paige's daughter has a big case. If I take it, it's going to cost her a lot."

"Can you do it pro-bono?" I ask before I offer to pay his damn fees. It's not like he needs the money, for fucks sake.

"Not this case. It will be a lengthy case. I'll need other lawyers to file for me since I can't go to court. She's unemployed, her parents are in debt, and I haven't read the lawsuits," he explains to me. "I can't keep accepting casseroles as a method of payment."

"She could be our nanny," Leyla suggests. "Paige always tells us about her amazing babysitting skills."

"Hadley is helping Paige with the bakery and attending to her dad, who, as you know, was in a bad car accident," I say, hoping to stop her before she gets ahead of herself.

"What happened to Paige's employees?" Pierce asks.

"She let them go around the same time she sold me the goats," Leyla answers, then smirks. "We could offer her the nanny job in exchange for a lot of services. They need medical and legal services. We could hire a couple of employees for the bakery through The Lodge and have them work at the bakery."

I shoot Pierce a look. "She is a genius. I still don't get why she's with you."

"Don't start irritating him," she says, pointing a finger at me "I don't have time for your nonsense. We should head home soon and discuss this plan with everyone. I think we found the perfect way to get ourselves a nanny."

"We're offering a lot in exchange," Pierce says.

I'm about to open my big mouth and offer to cover the cost of everything she needs when Leyla saves me. "She's going to be watching five children. I think it's fair. Sophia's twins are going to be a handful. We still have nine and a half months to go."

"She has a point," is all I say.

A COUPLE OF HOURS LATER, we are finally home with the rest of my brothers and sisters-in-law. Pierce waits until we are having dinner to bring up Leyla's genius idea. Everyone stays quiet while he gives them a summary of what he knows about Hadley's case, her parent's situation—which we already knew—and the cost of her expenses.

We could help her by asking her to help us. It's simple. Almost like a two-plus-two math problem. Only things are never simple at home. Henry is the first one to protest.

"We need to run a background check," Henry says. "The woman broke the trust of her employer. If she is taking care of our children, she could be telling shit to her mom and the rest of the town."

"You don't know her," I snap.

He glares at me, his jaw twitches. He's about to lose his shit. "And you're an expert on all things Hadley?"

I know a lot more than him, but I'm not getting into that discussion. At least, not today.

"No, but I'm giving her the benefit of the doubt. This might be the only way to get someone to help us with the kids." I tilt my head toward Sophia. "You have not one, but two children on the way. What are you going to do?"

Sophia rubs her belly. "I like her. If I had caught my boyfriend having sex, I'd have done the same or worse. She has the power of social media. She used it in her favor."

Pierce scowls. "Who uses her powers to fuck a rich asshole?"

"It doesn't matter, just fix it," I insist. It almost sounds like an order.

"Why would you care?" Henry's inquisitive glare is unnerving.

There are many answers to this question. Saying that I care too much about Hadley is one but there's another just as important. Only a few know what happened when I played for The Troopers. Beacon is one of them. I take several deep breaths to keep the anger at bay. It still makes my blood boil.

"They traded me to the Orcas when I was a rookie because Randall found me kissing his stepmother. Except I wasn't kissing her, she was groping me. I was only twenty-two with no support, so I just let the family shove me to Vancouver when I should have accused her of harassment."

"Screw them." Henry's tone is sharp and angry. "They messed with our little brother. They can pay through this chick."

Hayes sighs. "Vance, can you run a background check on Hadley? We'll need to interview her, and once we all agree that she's a good candidate, we can offer her the job. I'm sorry to hear that the Troopers traded you. I'm angry to learn that the woman took advantage of you. Is it possible to file a lawsuit?"

"I don't want to file a suit. I want you to defend Hadley and screw them in the process." The anger building in my gut isn't just because of what happened to me. I am still resentful. However, I want Pierce to dedicate his time to Hadley. Yes, I'm angry when I remember but I also moved on. "I don't want you to feel bad about what happened. I already worked through this with my therapist. I'm not disregarding the severity, just letting it go."

"But if you can get a little vengeance, that might help you with those underlying issues?" Pierce asks.

It wouldn't be vengeance as much as making sure they stop using their fucking money to get away with everything. "Yes, it'd make me feel better."

"Why do I feel like there's too much testosterone in this house?" Sophia complains.

"It's just another day in the Aldridge family. They always want to take someone down while helping others. They're like the modern Robin Hoods of Baker's Creek," Leyla laughs. "You better have at least one girl, or I swear I'm returning those children."

"There has never been an Aldridge girl," Henry states. "I wouldn't hold my breath if I were you."

"That's impossible," Blaire complains. "Maybe before you guys started keeping track, there was an Aldridge girl."

"It's not like we know everything about the Aldridge family," I remind them. "Remember Paige talking about our Dad working in the shop when she was young? She mentioned he was way different."

"Before we get side-tracked from this meeting, are we going to hire Hadley?" Pierce interrupts us.

"We should vote," Hayes suggests.

"Beacon isn't here," I remind them. "We should call him."

Hayes facetimes him immediately. Grace, his girlfriend, answers the phone.

"Hey, everyone," she says with a bright smile and a cheery voice. Her expression is so different from the one she had while my brother was in a coma. "I thought we weren't facetiming until Sunday."

"We might've found a nanny," Hayes tells her. "We need to vote."

"Where did you find her?" Beacon asks and Grace moves the camera toward him.

Relief slackens my bones when I notice that his face is no longer swollen. He's even smiling. If we're lucky, he'll be home in a few weeks.

Hayes explains to them everything about Hadley, including the lawsuit.

"We watched the video a couple of weeks ago," Beacon says.

"The wife, or whoever was in the background sounded upset. You could use that video for the defense."

"If it's still up," Pierce states.

"We will find it for you," Beacon offers. "We'll recruit G's brother. He's a genius when it comes to disappearing and reappearing posts that are floating in cyberspace."

"That's beside the point," I interrupt. "Are we hiring Hadley or not?"

We all vote in favor of interviewing her tomorrow before we hire her, as long as her background check comes squeaky clean. Sophia announces that they are building a nursery for Arden and the twins in one of the empty offices, letting everyone know that Easton's people will start next week. I hope that Hadley will be able to travel to Happy Springs to help us often, or at least, as often as we need her. I'm not sure how often that'll happen since Blaire and Layla will need help with Carter and Machlan.

When the meeting is over, Vance approaches me and says, "You're playing with fire."

Normally, I would tell him to fuck off. His insistence bothers me more than I want to let him know. I ignore him, taking Arden out of his highchair. Vance is wrong. This might be the best thing I could do for Hadley, even if it's the last.

Chapter Thirteen

Hadley

AS AGREED, I'm at the doorstep of a quaint little house that serves as the law office of Aldridge & Brassard Attorneys at Law. I spoke with Persy last night. She had no idea I was from Baker's Creek, but she's glad that Pierce Aldridge is looking into my case. I didn't tell her that he might not help me. I'm trying to stay optimistic about the outcome.

When the door opens, my heart skips a beat. It's Mills.

"I waited for you last night. We had something to discuss," he mumbles.

I realize that that's not what I wanted to hear. I was hoping for an *I miss you*. Not that he even should. We're just two people who happen to find each other at night and exchange a few kisses.

"I was in a bad place," I whisper, as I enter the house. "In fact, now I'm in a terrible place."

This arrangement of late-night talks and long kisses isn't working well for me. I'm enjoying them, but the last time I enjoyed the company of a man, I got screwed. He went back to his ex-wife, and he's now suing me.

Because you didn't think before you posted, my brain spits at me. Can't even get sympathy from my own thoughts.

Mills reaches my for hand and gives it a squeeze. "It's going to be okay."

That's easy for him to say. He doesn't get the gravity of my situation. I'm trying hard to stay positive, but my positivity is in the same range as my bank account at single digits. By tomorrow, I'm going to get a call from the bank letting me know I owe them money. I don't, I've barely even used my debit card, but life keeps finding a way to fuck me over.

"So why are you here?" I ask.

"We're waiting for you in the conference room," he states, drawing air quotes with his fingers.

I follow him toward the dining room and am a little nervous to see a lot of people staring at me.

My palms begin to sweat. What is this? The Spanish Inquisition? I wanted legal advice, not the round table of judgment. My mother is more than enough– she's not even speaking to me after what I told her yesterday and I refuse to apologize for finally telling her how I feel. Thankfully, she needs me enough to keep me around, or else I'd probably be in my car until she forgives me.

"Okay, let's introduce Hadley to everyone," Mills says. "Hadley, from your left to your right, this is Blaire, Hayes, Vance, you already met Sophia, Henry, Leyla, and Pierce."

"It's nice to meet you, everyone."

Mills pulls out a chair. "Please take a seat."

I do as he says. He sits on the chair beside mine. My nerves calm slightly by just having him right next to me. Is it crazy that being around him makes me giddy and gives me a sense of peace? We spend the first twenty minutes discussing children. I'm so intimidated by them that I keep answering everything they ask without hesitation.

Henry clears his throat. "I think we've heard enough."

"Why did you ask me all these questions? I am here to see if Pierce is going to be representing me, aren't I?" At least that's what I hoped would happen. It just occurs to me that this feels like a job interview rather than a legal consultation. Why is everyone here?

Henry's furrow in his eyebrows deepens when he tells Pierce with a low, demanding voice. "She has to sign it before we can continue this meeting."

Pierce, who sits to my right, hands me a folder. "That's a non-disclosure agreement."

I open and read it. I'm not allowed to discuss the family business with anyone, share pictures of the children or them on social media. "This is ridiculous," I complain. "Why would I sign something like this?"

"We have a proposal," Mills says. "But we can't discuss it until you sign it."

I look at him, waiting for more, but he's staring at the table. Maybe this is what he needed to talk about last night. I wish I had gone to the park. I wanted it more than anything. How odd is it to need someone who I just met? It is unsettling and wonderful all at once. If I met him last night I could've made a mistake like started to fall in love with him. I'm too vulnerable to be fooling around with him.

Even though my thoughts about him are scattered, I can stop them and focus on this NDA. Why would they need me to sign it? If this will help me fix at least one part of the chaos that has become my life, I'll do it.

"What the hell," I mumble. "It's not like I'm going to lose anything by signing it."

The second I'm done signing, Henry says, "We need someone to help us take care of our kids. We can't pay you."

I laugh humorlessly. "So you want me to do it for free?"

"Yes. Pierce, can you please give the contract to her?" He answers, and Pierce hands me a second folder. "If you nanny for our five children, we will pay your father's medical bills, your legal fees, and your mother's expenses."

The deal sounds great, but this wouldn't work for me. I would love to give them a hand, but do they realize how much they need to pay? I'm hopeful, and yet, I feel like I'm missing something. Now, if they plan on paying everything…who offers that much to a stranger?

"That doesn't make sense. Why would you do that? Wouldn't it be easier to pay me? I can't rent an apartment from imaginary money."

"We can amend it and provide housing," Mills states. "I'll take care of that since she's also taking care of Arden. We could give her a credit card and petty cash to cover our children's expenses—and hers."

"I still don't understand why you're doing this. Wouldn't it be easier if you pay me?"

"You can't tell anyone about this deal," Pierce warns me, ignoring my questions. "Not even your parents. Do you understand?"

"Of course, I just signed your NDA."

Hayes tells me about their father's will, the stipulations, and most of the nonsense they need to do in order to receive their inheritance. They had to move to Baker's Creek after William Aldridge's death and they aren't allowed to leave for eighteen months. That explains their sudden presence. They need to dedicate their time to The Lodge, the factory, and the town.

If either one of them leaves without the permission of some

lawyer, it'll be considered a violation of the will. They can't hire people to do house chores, like taking care of the barn, the animals, or cleaning the house. Only family and friends can take care of their children. My blood freezes when he says that if any of the stipulations aren't met, everything owned by the Aldridges will be sold and destroyed. That means my mother's bakery and my parents' house.

My eyes open wide. I'm in such a state of shock that it takes me a few seconds to respond.

"That'll destroy the town."

They all nod.

"You can't tell anyone," Henry warns me. "We don't know how the people of the town will react if they learn about any of this. They shouldn't know why we're here."

"So once it's over, you're leaving, and what's going to happen to them?"

"Some of us are staying," Hayes says. "That's not the point of this conversation. We feel like you could be a good fit for us."

"You don't know me," I answer immediately. "Just because you threw a bunch of questions at me, it doesn't mean I'm qualified."

"Your mom told us that you were the best babysitter in town."

"Mom tends to embellish the truth a little."

"So, you've never taken care of a kid?" Henry asks.

It's not like I'm trying to sabotage this weird job interview, but what if I get a real job? Being a nanny isn't my vocation. I'm not going to stay here for a year or whatever time they need me. Why should I? My mom is ashamed of me, she can't wait to see me leave. She'd rather be handling this mess on her own than to keep me around.

"What if I get a job offer and I need to leave?"

"We'll figure that out when it happens," Mills answers. "Arden is a good judge of character and he likes you."

If he's trying to butter me up, it's working.

I am delighted to know that Arden likes me. He's a wonderful kid who I'd love to spend more time with, and it makes me feel good knowing Mills trusts me with his kid. So why am I hesitating? Maybe I believe that I don't deserve this break.

"This is a great opportunity, but can I think about it?"

My answer might not be what they expect, but it's all I can offer until I have time to think it over, and maybe discuss it with my parents.

Chapter Fourteen

Hadley

ON MY WAY TO MY PARENTS' house, my phone rings a loud trill that I know to ignore. If there's something I've learned from this town, it's to never answer your phone in the middle of Main Street. If you do, your entire phone conversation will end up online somewhere. I didn't learn that from experience, but I've seen it happen several times. Even when I lived in another state, I'd still browse the town's social media. It's somehow fascinating to watch how fast they are at posting and spreading their so-called news.

When I arrive at home, I check my missed calls. Randall's name appears twice.

"Good luck getting me to answer, asshole," I mumble.

I check on Dad, who is thankfully sleeping. The hospital bed that the doctor lent us has been a godsend. I know Hayes Aldridge denied it, but he was the one who paid the contractor to make this house handicap accessible. As I cover Dad with another blanket, I decide to accept the job. The Aldridges have more money than the entire town put together. They can afford to pay for everything my family needs while I help them with their kids. It's not like I have anything more important to do.

Someone has to ensure that they complete the will's stipulations. If they take away my parent's house and the bakery, they won't have anything left. I kiss Dad's temple and head out. I stop right by the door frame where Mom used to measure my height. This place has a lot more than a few memories. I grew up here.

Maybe after all this is over, I can convince them to sell us the house. If I have a real job by then, I might be able to apply for a mortgage.

When I grab the doorknob, my phone rings again. I check it, and I'm not surprised when I see Randall's face flashing. I decline the call and wiggle the door open, but the asshole calls one more time.

I give in and answer the phone. "Yes?"

"Hadley, babe," he greets me.

I'm not his babe. "What do you want, Randall?"

He clears his throat. "I miss you. Can you come home?"

I bark out a laugh. He is priceless. "Are you drunk, high, or did you hit your head? Yesterday I got served with not one but two lawsuits, and today you're asking me to go back home."

He doesn't say a word. The only sound on the other line is his breath.

"I'm going to hang up, and you're going to lose my number."

"It's nothing personal," he mumbles. "My family. Well, you know them."

He's got to be kidding me. "It is personal. I don't have a penny to my name."

"You tampered with my image and the image of the team," he groans and I imagine him scrubbing his face in frustration the way he always does.

I wish I could tell him he deserved it, but if he's recording this call, it would make everything worse than it already is.

"I miss you," he says with a voice that used to send shivers down my spine, but now it makes me cringe. "I'm all alone."

"Suzie isn't enough?" Okay, I'm petty, but yeah, is one woman not enough for him?

"If you apologize to my family, I'll forgive you. I'll even give you your job back," he offers, ignoring my question.

"How drunk are you?" He doesn't sound drunk, but then again, some people sound pretty sober while they are under the influence.

"My life sucks because of you. My uncle wants to fire me. My parents want to kick me out of my apartment. I need you to come back and fix this."

What is wrong with him? As time passes, I'm coming to the realization that I was dating a very immature man. We got along well when I was twenty-six because we had the same mental age, but one of us is stuck in his mid-twenties, and that's not me.

"Lose my number," I repeat and hang up the phone.

As I'm about to leave the house, Mom is making her way toward me. I check the time, and it's past four. She could have stayed open for another thirty minutes if I had arrived on time. Fucking Randall. He screws up everything.

"Hey, Mom," I greet her, closing the door behind her.

"I heard you went to visit Pierce Aldridge," she pauses. "Again. He's married."

"Mom, are you insinuating that I'm trying to sleep with him?"

"Not at all, but the rumors started. You need to stay away from those men, mostly the married ones. This town thrives on gossip, and I don't want to hear them say that you are sleeping with any of them."

I don't know how to take her comment. Is she calling me a harlot or preventing a catastrophe?

"As I mentioned when I left the bakery, I had a job interview," I remind her.

She takes a step backward, and the look in her eyes says she's about to go ballistic. "You had an interview with them? Not at The Lodge? That is different. Rita, the human resources manager is the one who does the hiring. Not the brothers."

"Well, since you like to brag about my babysitting skills to anyone that will listen, the Aldridge family wanted to see if I'd be interested in taking care of their children."

She frowns, shakes her head, and takes off her sweater. It's not often that Mom is speechless. She always has something to say. Not today.

"They offered me a job."

"You can't live on a babysitting salary. I can understand the appeal of getting twenty dollars a night for looking after a couple of toddlers when you were a teenager." She keeps her voice low but still sharp and probably angry. Her face is darkening slightly. She's about to lose her shit, walk away, and stop talking to me again.

"They are paying me slightly more than twenty bucks per day," I answer, trying to figure out how I'm going to tell her that they'll be making her life easier for the next nine to twelve months.

"Will they be okay if you only work a couple of evenings?"

"There's no set schedule. They want me to be the nanny, which implies working for them almost twenty-four hours a day, seven days a week. We didn't talk about time off. It seems like a lot, but there's downtime because though they want me available to them, they won't need me all the time. The salary is low, but they are giving me some discounts on the medical supplies Dad requires and they plan to work something out with the hospital to reduce

Dad's bills. They plan to lend you a couple of employees from The Lodge and send one of the nurses they employ to help Dad. I think that should help."

"No," she says. "You can't work for them. It'll take you away from the bakery."

"You'll get two people to help you. Do you need more? I'll be out of your way. Maybe I'll save enough money so that I can leave town."

"You can't wait to run away from this town, can you? Are you ashamed of your family or the entire town? We're not rich, but we paid for your education. I tried my best to—"

"Mom, I'm not ashamed of you. I don't like the way everyone treats me in this town." I pause to take a deep breath so I can keep a calm tone. The last thing I want is to fight with her. "You never noticed, but I've always been an outcast. The Marys bullied me. Why would I want to stay?"

"Why didn't you tell me?" The shock on her face is priceless.

"Add it to the list of disappointments?" I shake my head.

"You don't disappoint me. I'm proud of you. Your dad and I are proud of you. I never thought it would affect you that I made things up. You live in another state. I don't like them to know our real business. I keep the things that matter to myself—you are precious to us."

"Well, while you were doing that, you made me feel like shit."

She huffs out a breath. "I never thought it would affect you. I love you, Hadley. You're the most important thing in the world. You have no idea how relieved I was that you were your own person while growing up."

Mom pauses, looks around, blows out a breath, and leans her hip on the back of the couch. The storm in her eyes is gone just like the tension in her back. Her voice is gentler when she says, "I don't want you to leave, but we'll keep visiting you if you have to. You don't have to sacrifice yourself and work for the Aldridges. Though, I'd love it if you take over the bakery when I retire. It's our family's heritage. I hope that one day you can pass it to your daughter."

"We'll talk about it when it's time, but for now, I need to figure out how we as a family are going to get through this rough patch, Mom. The job they offered me will not only help you, but it'll help me. Pierce Aldridge is going to work my case pro-bono."

The twin lines between her eyebrows smooth away as she takes in a deep breath. "What kind of trouble did you get yourself in, Hadley?"

"I told you Randall cheated. What I didn't tell you is that I posted his picture on social media, and now he's throwing a tantrum. His family has money, and they're trying to make an example out of me."

"Working for the Aldridges might bring you more trouble than you want to admit. A lot of women are trying to date the single ones. You might become the talk of the town. I don't want that to happen to you."

"I'm a big girl, Mom. I can take a few months of gossip and bullying."

"I love you. You're a good kid, Hadley."

"Love you too, Mom," I say, hugging her and feeling that we smoothed a problem we ignored for years.

Chapter Fifteen

Hadley

"I WASN'T sure if you'd be here," Mills says as I approach our bench.

"This and the wooded area on the north side of the Aldridge mansion are my favorite places. Though, I can't get into the property anymore. The owners might not like it if I break and enter," I whisper conspiratorially. "You can hang out in my secret spot since you own the place and leave me to my bench."

He laughs for a moment. "Do you want to go to the underground apartment?"

"No. The last time we were there, I almost lost my clothes, and you were fully dressed. You don't play fair," I say teasingly.

"What if I promise to keep my hands to myself?"

"Do I get to watch while you're playing *with yourself*?" I gasp and cover my mouth. "Sorry, I got carried away."

He doesn't need his hands to undress me. His intense gaze is doing it without even touching me. I squeeze my legs together, my core pulsing as the lust that he carries charges the atmosphere with an unattainable desire.

This has to stop.

The kisses and the light touches.

The loving caresses and the unsaid words.

The need to be filled in all those empty places in my heart, body, and soul.

Every time his lips touch my skin, it feels as if his heart speaks softly to mine. I want this, but I don't want it at all. I don't know him. He makes me vulnerable. He makes me act without thinking about the consequences.

Neither one of us can afford to make mistakes.

There are too many outside factors to consider. He has a beautiful son who needs my attention. He's going to be my employer. Neither one of us can afford the gossip of this town.

My heart can't afford to be broken.

"I missed you last night," he says with a low voice that feels like a gentle caress to my soul.

He doesn't need his hands to touch me. It's taking a lot of self-control not to say, "yes, lead the way."

"We have to stop," I repeat even when my lips, my body, and my soul want the opposite. "Come tomorrow, this is going to become forbidden, or at least frowned upon. I can't afford to do anything stupid."

"So, you're accepting the job?"

After a second or two, I nod. "You guys made it almost impossible to say no. I need everything that you're offering."

I'm still planning on doing some social media consulting and handling some accounts. This job sounds perfect, but it has an expiration date. The kisses we share melt my insides, yet, they're only stolen moments we can't hold onto.

It's so frustrating to go from a stagnant life to...what can I even call this?

A transition where I got to taste the most delicious kisses in the world. The strongest arms that can encircle my body and make me feel safe.

How can a man be capable of producing so many emotions at once?

When I look into Mills's dark green eyes, I wonder if he can see the similar positions we're in. We're both so empty that we're trying to feed each other's loneliness. In other circumstances, I'd give in to whatever it is that we've been doing, but my heart can't afford to fall in love with a mistake.

A hot mistake who stands up, leans closer to me to whisper smoothly in my ear. "Can I ask for just one last kiss?"

"You could, but I won't say yes," I mutter, almost breathless. He's too close. His heat threatens to ignite my body.

What is it about him that makes me want to say "fuck the world" and let him take me? I'm usually more cautious, but with him, I dive in without even thinking. Nothing in my head makes sense, except for him.

He grabs my hand, entwining our fingers. I love the way they fit together. "Please," he begs. "One last kiss before this gets too complicated. Before I'm not allowed to do this." He runs his lips along my jaw. My heart races as his mouth sears heat along my skin and almost touches my soul.

"I should say no." I breathe the words as his teeth scrape my skin.

This is farewell to these late nights and those heart-melting, toe-curling, spontaneously orgasmic kisses. This should be simple. We're both consenting adults. But I know that I'm not thinking straight. I'm still getting over my last relationship. I didn't love Randall, but the guy hurt me nonetheless. Mills is no ordinary man. He's a famous hockey player, my future employer, and one of the men who can destroy my family if I piss him off. It would be so effortless, saying yes to this offer. We could run to the private apartment, and in less than five minutes, I'll be pinned against the wall, his big hands sliding down my body. His mouth will capture mine, and we'll devour each other. He'll press his hips against mine, and I'll crave more. There won't be any way back from that point. I just know that if I let this happen tonight, I'll destroy the only chance I have to save my family.

"No," I say, kissing his cheek and separating our hands. It's so painful to move away from him, but I can't risk my future—or my heart. "We shouldn't do this."

"Had," he says, his voice trembling.

"You understand it's for the best, don't you?" I try to bargain with him. "I like these late-night talks. It feels like I have a friend in town. I'm not ready to lose that."

He nods.

"See you around."

I turn tail and run toward my house, legs pumping in order to stop myself from going back to claim that kiss or to accept his tempting invitation.

When I arrive home, I lock the door of my room behind me and lean against it, a few stray tears running down my cheeks. I hate crying, but I can't help myself. I'm angry at life. It's so fucking unfair. Why can't I meet a man like Mills outside of Baker's Creek?

There has to be a guy like him somewhere in the world that kisses just the way I need him to kiss me. A man who desires me just for being me. Not because he's lonely or…

I dab the tears with the sleeve of my sweatshirt. It hurts now, but the anger will be gone in the morning, and solutions to my problems will rise with the sun.

I SPEND the first four hours of the morning helping Mom before I head to check on Dad who is, thankfully, asleep. The doctor said they are going to start weaning him off of the pain medications next Monday. I hope that by then, we have a nurse ready for him.

At nine, I head to Pierce's office.

When I knock on the door, Mills is the one behind it.

"Hey," he greets me.

"Do you guys have a moment?"

He nods, opening the door wide.

"Good, she's here," a female voice says.

I assume it's Leyla because she has auburn hair. She comes almost running toward me and hands me a screaming baby. "This is Carter. He's teething, and he needs someone else to carry him because everyone else in the Aldridge family is tired." She looks around the room. "The surgery won't take me more than an hour. I trust you guys will handle everything."

With that, she leaves the room.

"Is she a doctor?" I ask.

I bounce the baby as I walk to where I believe is the kitchen.

"Veterinarian," Pierce corrects me, following me. "Is it safe to assume that you came to accept the position?"

I grab a clean kitchen towel to wrap around an ice cube, and rub it carefully along Carter's gums. Once he starts calming himself, I turn to look at Pierce, "Yes. I hope it's okay if I start next Monday. Mom and Dad still need help. I don't know when you'll be able to get anyone to hire the new employees for the bakery or to hire a nurse to assist dad."

He looks at his son and then at me. "Am I deaf, or did he stop crying?"

I hand the baby over to him, along with the kitchen towel. "My grandma would've suggested some whiskey on the gums," I shrug.

"Can you stay today?"

As I'm about to answer, a little ball of energy comes running toward me, yelling "Mama!"

"Hadley," I correct him, squatting. "How are you today?"

"Hawley," he says, clinging to my neck. "You back!"

"You give the best hugs in the world," I tell him, standing up and picking him up from the floor. "What have you been up to since the last time we saw each other?"

He frowns, looking at me intently.

"Did you have breakfast today?"

He gives me a sharp nod. "Baffes."

"I like pancakes more than waffles. Maybe the next time I visit your house, we can try to make some chocolate pancakes," I offer.

"Pway?"

"Miss Hadley is busy today with Carter," Pierce says.

I look up at him and shake my head. "I can't take care of them today."

"You can't leave me with them. I'm just one man," he says with a desperate plea.

I scan the living room. "Where is Mills?"

"He had a meeting at The Lodge," he answers. "He was just leaving when you came in. He, Sophia, and Henry are pulling a few people out of The Lodge's gift shop and the restaurant to help your mom today. They'll be hiring a few people who will work exclusively for the bakery and in the meantime, they'll send some of the current employees. We assume that she doesn't want a baker with her, does she?"

I stare at him, processing everything he just said. Before I can respond he continues. "Part of your contract includes housing. There's a little place two houses to the left of the mansion. It belongs to the family, but it's been neglected like many things that belonged to my father. Easton will update the kitchen, recarpet the floors, and paint the walls. Sophia and Leyla will furnish it, especially since they set up a nursery and a playroom for the kids, in case you needed to care for them overnight."

I'm surprised at how fast this family is working to give me what they promised. They are providing me with not just a room, but a house. Mom and I are only two people. If she gets more employees, she'll have more time to spend baking. I said I'll be back in a few, but if they are covering the bakery and they let me take the kids to my house I can help them. We'll benefit if I accept today.

"If you let me take them to my house so I can watch my Dad, I can be with them for a couple of hours," I offer.

He smiles. "You're the best. If I could give you a raise, I would."

"I can think of other ways you can repay me, like giving my dad his goats back," I counter with a smirk.

He brings out a stroller from the coat closet and gives me a diaper bag. "It has everything either one of them might need. When you bring them back, you can sign the contract. Remember, you're a friend of ours and you're doing this because you want to help us, not because we're hiring you.

Chapter Sixteen

Mills

HADLEY CHANGED OUR LIVES.

That's the overall consensus in the house. She's a lifesaver. After four weeks, the home runs smoothly. During this time, I've discovered two things. One: we need her more than we need coffee. Which we didn't think was possible since this entire house runs on caffeine. Well, except Blaire and Sophia who can't drink any right now. Two: with her taking care of the kids, we have more time to concentrate on work. Don't get me wrong, I'm not neglecting my son. It just means that I get to work for five to seven hours straight, and then go home to spend the rest of the day with him, uninterrupted.

When my father died, I thought moving to Baker's Creek was a dumb idea. I knew it would affect Arden in one way or another especially if my brothers wouldn't try to connect with him. I was wrong. This is precisely what he needed, what we both needed. Our schedule in Vancouver was out of the ordinary. I'd drop him at daycare while I was training, and a babysitter or one of the hockey wives would watch him during games. He traveled everywhere with me.

A year ago when Beacon was trying to convince me to move to Baker's Creek and not let the town down, he mentioned Arden needed a routine and I needed a break. He was partially right. We needed a break from that life. But now that we're here, I can't help thinking about what's next for the two of us. I know it's not Baker's Creek, and it's definitely not Hadley. We offered her a contract for a year. Eleven months left of Hadley, until she leaves us for better things. She's here for the whole family, but it's me and Arden that she'll be leaving.

I shouldn't be concerned about the ending of that contract, but it's going to be really fucking hard to explain to my son that Hadley isn't part of our life anymore. I'm not looking forward to the moment when we pack and leave. Maybe I should make a few changes to his schedule so he doesn't get too attached.

They spend too much time together. Hadley only has all three of the boys in the morning. After eleven, she focuses all her time on Arden, who adores her. He thinks she is *his* Hadley. At least he doesn't call her Mama anymore.

Watching them interact is sweet and torturous. She's patient, gentle, and sweet with him. The best part of my day is when I arrive in time to watch her read him a story. Her voice is so soothing that he falls right to sleep. I love seeing my son when I come back from work, but I love it more when I can catch those special moments.

I should avoid her the same way children avoid brussels sprouts. I just can't be too far from her. We keep a good enough distance that neither one of us is tempted to reach out to the other and do something that we'll both regret.

She owes me a kiss that I might never claim. Maybe she'll make an exception for the last day we're both in Baker's Creek. I don't know where I'll be going or what I'll be doing, but I'm sure we'll be heading in different directions. If I go back to play, Arden's life is going to shift again. I want him to have a normal life, something different from what I experienced.

Most of all, I want him to be happy. I just need to find what it is that'll make him happy.

When I enter the house, the sound of his giggle fills the air and my heart. He's playing with Hadley on the setup we have in the living room. For one second, a stupid thought crosses my mind. What if Hadley and I stay in Baker's Creek? Together? What if she's the one who makes us happy? Could we make her happy?

"You came a little earlier," Sophia says from behind me. I look over my shoulder, startled by her voice. My sisters-in-law are like ghosts. They appear out of nowhere and scare me shitless all the time. "You Aldridge men are weird."

"How so?"

"Every time you're falling in love, you guys behave like idiots and avoid the woman who holds your interest," she snickers.

My brows lift. I swear these women confuse the fuck out of me all the time. "What are you talking about?"

"More like who am I talking about." She tilts her head toward the mat where Had and Arden are playing. "Hadley. You have a crush on her. If you avoid her, you might avoid falling in love. Let me know how that works out."

I laugh and shrug out of my jacket. "You're wrong."

I can tell from her mischievous grin that she thinks I'm full of shit.

I'm not.

I like Hadley. Do I enjoy kissing her? Yes, she's delicious. Would I want to see how well her naked body fits against mine? Based on all the dreams I've had about her, it's safe to say yes.

That only means I want to have sex with her. There are no feelings between us.

"If that's what helps you sleep at night." She grins widely, confident in her judgment.

"The day we interviewed her, you were her biggest supporter. Once she signed the dotted line, you started avoiding her. Your brothers think that you don't like her. We know better. You like her," she nudges me with her shoulder. "A lot."

"By we, do you mean, you and your unborn children?"

She laughs. "No. Ley, Blaire, and me. Grace would agree if she saw you. I'll bring her up to date soon."

These women are nosy and dangerous. I just hope Hadley doesn't become one of them. "I'm not going to have this conversation with you."

"Dad!" Arden says, pointing at me.

Hadley looks up and smiles. That gorgeous smile knocks me off my feet and makes me want to bend down and meet her lips with mine. I ignore Sophia and march to where they are.

"Hey, sport," I greet my son, taking him into my arms and twirling him a couple of times before I give him a big hug. "How was your day?"

"I was with Hady, Papa Dick, and Cato."

"He's still not saying Hadley, huh?" I say casually to her.

She shrugs. "He'll get there."

Arden talks a lot more than he did before Hadley came to us. It's impressive how much he can mumble, not that it's all easy to understand. I'm guessing it's because Hadley talks a lot too.

Though I want to avoid looking at her beautiful brown eyes, I finally turn to meet her gaze. "Thank you for spending some time with him."

"It's my favorite time of the day," she says, standing up and dusting her jeans.

"So still no luck in calling your dad, Papa Rick, huh?"

She shakes her head a couple of times. "Nope. Carter is still Cato. He's speaking a lot, though. Earlier, we went to the bakery for some dough, and he had a long conversation with Mom."

"Why would you need dough?"

She glances toward the kitchen. "We made cookies. I thought it'd be easier to grab some of the dough I made earlier today than make some from scratch. Good luck with dinner."

"Why?"

She smirks. "I promised he could eat the cookies he decorated."

I'm about to tell her that she has to stay for dinner when Pierce enters the house. "Is Hadley still around?" He calls, loudly.

"What happened?" she asks, alarmed.

"Do you have a moment? We need to talk about your case." He says, pulling some files from his portfolio.

She flinches. "How bad is it?"

"Oh, there's nothing new, we just might be able to settle. We have a zoom meeting with your ex's lawyers tomorrow. There's going to be a mediator." He turns his attention from Hadley to me. "You need to take a few hours off or find someone to take care of Arden. It's Friday, so Leyla will be with Carter. And I think tomorrow is Hayes's day off, so he can take care of Machlan."

"It's the day I go to Aldry's but I can work from here," I say.

Since Sophia conditioned one of the offices to be a nursery and another to be a playroom, Friday is one of my favorite days. I get to drive Arden to Aldry's. Hadley meets us there so she can help me look after him while I'm in meetings or conference calls. Tomorrow I can just stay at home. I'm glad that Hadley has this meeting, but I hate that I won't be able to take her and Arden for lunch like I planned.

"Where do you want to talk about the case? I need to prep you," Pierce asks her.

"We could go to my place, or we can use the dining room," she suggests.

"Are you okay if they listen to our conversation?" Pierce asks.

"It's not like I have anything to hide," She shrugs.

AROUND ELEVEN, when everyone is already in bed, I head toward the park. I couldn't listen to Pierce and Hadley's conversation because he kicked everyone out of the house until only the dogs were left. Hadley didn't have a problem, but he did.

When I arrive at the bench, she's there working on her laptop. "I knew you'd be here."

"I'm that predictable, huh?"

"You seem to gravitate toward it when you're restless," I answer.

"If there's anything I missed during college, it was this park," she sighs.

"Just during college?"

"I got used to not having an entire park where I could hang out until midnight," she explains while typing. "But whenever I leave, I'm taking this bench with me."

"You're going to steal the bench?" I ask, laughing.

"It's mine," she argues, and her voice comes out quite adorable —a combination of tiredness and excitement that only Hadley can muster.

"In what dimension can you claim a public bench?"

"Are you going to stop me?" She raises a brow, playfully daring me.

"Nah, I might help you load it," I answer because clearly, she's fixating on the bench to avoid another subject. "Why don't you tell me why you're here?"

She glances back at the screen and then at me. "The question is, why are you here? Your brother is back. He seems to be doing well, or at least, everyone in the house says he's doing a lot better than they expected. I have yet to meet him or his girlfriend."

She's deflecting from herself. I could continue the conversation and tell her that Beacon is doing a lot better than many doctors expected.

"I came to make sure that you're okay."

"Never been better. How about you?"

"I'm concerned. You have a face-to-face meeting with your ex and his lawyers tomorrow."

She closes her laptop with a deep sigh, humoring me. "We have a plan. I'll apologize for having a mental lapse since it was painful to realize that Randall didn't love me anymore. He likes when I stroke his ego. They'll back off because they don't want to drag his name through the mud."

I'm sure there's a lot more to what she's saying, but I let the subject go. Her intention for tonight is to forget that she's still dealing with the Quintons. If what she needs is a distraction, I can give her that.

"If you have a pair of ice skates, I can take you to the ice rink. It's one hundred percent functional. So far, I'm the only one who has tested it."

"I've never owned a pair of skates. The last time I ice skated, I was thirteen." She points toward Mount Hood. "I would say let's go skiing, but there's no snow, and it's too dark. You should teach Arden to skate, though. Isn't that like a rule among hockey players to teach your kid to skate before they walk?"

I huff, rolling my eyes. "That's ridiculous. I do want to teach Arden how to skate, though. I need to drive to Portland to buy him a pair of skates. You should come with us on Saturday."

We stare at each other for a long moment and I can see the gears turning in her head. "I shouldn't," she says. "We've handled our situation well enough. If we can keep it up for the next eight to eleven months..." Her voice trails off, and so does her gaze. "We need to keep this professional."

"There's no harm in going to Portland to choose a pair of skates. It's not like we can fuck in the car with my son coming along." I decide to use my best weapon to convince her. "Arden adores you. I'm sure he'd love to take his *Hadey* with him."

"The feeling is mutual. He's precious." She seems a little hesitant before she speaks again. "I've been meaning to ask... what happened with his mother?"

The question hits me like a puck hurtling at ninety miles per hour, and I don't have a mask on to avoid it or enough time to deflect it. It gets me right between my brows.

Fuck. I hate to talk about Margaret.

"Like you don't know," I mumble, trying to avoid the conversation.

It's public knowledge that I didn't marry her, and I have full custody of Arden. There's nothing else to it.

"I know what I've read, but that's not the friends and family version. If you don't want to tell me, it's okay," she says. "I just can't understand why she doesn't have contact with him. If I were his mother, I'd be devastated if he was so far away from me. Either you don't let her see him, or she doesn't care to see him."

"She didn't want him."

I open up to her about Margaret, reluctant to be so vulnerable but wanting to share the truth with her.

"She's missing the most wonderful boy in the world," she says earnestly, stealing a piece of my heart. "He's the most loving kid I've ever met. I live for his laughs, and I can't get enough of his kindness. How could she...? I'm sorry."

A lot of women have praised my son since he was born. I know that they were empty phrases to butter me up because no one has ever taken the time to actually get to know him. I know that Hadley gets paid to do it, but the way she interacts with him makes me... never mind. I need to stop thinking about the organs affected by her behavior toward Arden. There are many things that I have to avoid, and falling for Hadley Heywood is one of them. I offer to walk her home, and it takes all my strength not to kiss her or to beg her to invite me in. I need her as much as I need my next breath.

I guess I'll have to live with blue balls and disappointment.

Chapter Seventeen

Hadley

THE VIDEOCONFERENCE WITH THE LAWYERS, Randall, and his parents lasted almost two hours. Pierce was assertive. He made a lot of great points about my previous employment and gathered several witnesses who helped with both the case of Randall versus me, and The Troopers versus me. I mean, the guy not only got Randall to withdraw the lawsuit, he found three other women who were his lovers while we were dating. He made the Denver Troopers pay me for all the emotional damage I went through. He requested back payment since I was underpaid while holding a key position in the organization.

In the end, the team and Randall settled on a significant amount that solves my financial problems. I could pay the Aldridges and quit my job, but I won't. After a month of working with them, I've come to realize how much they're doing for the town. They may be staying to satisfy the stipulations of their father's will, but they don't have to put so much effort into helping the town grow. They put their lives on hold to make sure that the people of Baker's Creek and Happy Springs don't end up homeless because of their father. Not to mention, I love the kids so much, I'm not ready to leave them. Especially Arden, my favorite baby boy.

Since every child has their parent for the day, I go to my house. Home is now a small three-bedroom house on Rainier Lane and only a few doors from the Aldridge's mansion. It's been only a month but it feels more like home than any other place I've lived in since I left Baker's Creek. Right by the entrance there's an antique table I bought during one of the town's festivals. That's where I set a vase and a bouquet of paper pink, mauve, and purple flowers Mills had delivered a couple of weeks ago.

It had a thank you note from the Aldridges for all I've done for them. As a woman who has a big crush on him, I want to believe that he sent them because he was thinking of me. I hang up my purse on the hook next to the antique mirror that matches the table. I bought that online.

Today has been long and my black slacks, white button-down t-shirt, and heels feel more like custom than formal clothes. I need to change into something more comfortable but before that I decide to take a shower.

My bathroom is in the main bedroom, next to a big walk-in closet that holds only a few clothes and a lot of the boxes that I haven't unpacked just yet. After I take a shower, I change into a comfortable pair of jeans and a tank top. It's almost lunchtime, so I make my way back down the stairs. That's when I hear a knock on the door. When I check the peephole, it's two of my favorite guys. I open the door right away.

"Hadey!" Arden yells my name, capturing my legs.

"Hey, baby boy. I missed you." I lift him and hug him. He gives me a sloppy kiss on the cheek. "This is a nice surprise."

"Pierce said you were done with the meeting and that things went well," Mills answers. "I just wanted to check on you."

I open the door wide. "Do you want to come in? It might be better than staying by the door and giving the town something to talk about."

Just the other day a rumor spread that I'm going out with Vance. It was right after he flew Dad and me to Portland to take us to an appointment with the physical therapist since he couldn't travel to Baker's Creek this week. Any time I'm with an Aldridge, there's a rumor. Mom keeps asking me what's happening with them like she doesn't know I can't tell her anything. As though the NDA will disappear if she asks enough questions.

I walk into the house with Arden in my arms. Mills, who is right behind me, closes the door. "So, how was it?"

"It was better than I expected. They settled, and my bank account should be receiving a hefty amount by next week," I tell him.

"What are your plans?" He asks as a matter of fact. I've been interacting with him for several weeks. By now, I've noticed that when he's around his family he speaks a lot more than when it's just the two of us. As if while he is with others, his voice gets lost among his brothers and he won't be getting as much attention.

Is this like a middle child syndrome effect? Is he shy? Maybe he doesn't know how to interact with women beyond a one-night stand and he's just learning.

"I have a few ideas but no long-term plans yet," I confess. There's nothing I can do, at least for the next few months. I'll be buying the bakery and myself a new laptop. Well, one for each. Doing social media consulting is easy, and it pays well. It's something I can do anywhere. Could I even travel while working and wouldn't that be wonderful?

Arden rests his head on my chest. "Do you want milk and cookies, baby?"

He looks at me and nods once sharply. "Yez pease."

"We haven't had lunch yet," Mills protests.

"Do you want a sandwich?"

"Samich," Arden nods. "And cadots, and tootsies."

"Would you like to stay for lunch, or do you need to be at home?"

"We can stay."

Mills is looking at me strangely. I don't know how to interpret the look so I choose to ignore it.

Arden and I pull all the food to prepare the sandwiches while Mills peels and cuts some carrots. He washes and chops some strawberries too. Mills offers to wash the dishes once we're done, while Arden and I read a book. The house should be equipped with everything the children might need, so I take the chance to buy a book every week from my aunt who owns the bookstore. I like to be prepared for them, but mainly for Arden. Mills comes to the playroom after he's done, and we spend a few hours building weird creatures with blocks, drawing, and reading stories.

"I should take him home," Mills says, watching Arden's head begin to bounce.

"We have a toddler bed in the other room," I offer, taking him into my arms and carrying him into the kid's guestroom.

I'm not ready for them to leave. Today has been strange but special, and I don't want it to end just yet. I know they have to be at home between six and seven for supper with the family, and as I lay Arden down, I find myself wishing that this was my life. Mills as my partner and Arden as my son.

I know it's stupid to believe that maybe they can be part of me or I can be a part of them, but a girl can dream. At least for a couple of hours.

Mills looks at Arden, then at me. "Sorry, Had, we really should go."

"Okay," I say, trying to act like it doesn't hurt more than anything Randall ever did to me.

He takes two steps closer, our bare feet almost touching. He cups my cheek with his palm and plants a soft kiss on my lips that makes me shiver. Sometimes all it takes is for him to touch me, and I melt.

"I want you." He kisses my forehead. "I want you so fucking much that if I stay, I'm going to lose the last strand of self-control that I have. I'm going to drag you to your room, kiss you senseless and make you mine." His voice is deep, reserved.

"Tell me you understand, Had," he begs me. "If things were different—"

"I know," I whisper, but I really don't know what he means.

What does he mean by different?

"Come with us tomorrow," he asks again. "We'll have fun, I promise. Arden and I love to spend time with you."

"Okay," I say, finally giving in.

He kisses my temple and leaves.

THE NEXT MORNING, Mills texts me asking to meet at the mansion. I go through the back of the bakery to steal a few fresh croissants and walk to the coffee shop for coffee. Mills and his brothers run on caffeine. If they could, they would have an IV dripping coffee all day.

When I get close to the house, he's already setting Arden in his car seat.

"I was hoping we'd have some breakfast." I present the tray of coffee and the box of pastries.

"Get in before the land sharks see them, they'll pry them away from you," he warns me, laughing.

"Do they know you call them land sharks?"

"Do I look like I have a death wish?" he asks, opening the passenger door for me, holding the drink carrier and the box. He kisses my cheek. "Morning."

Once I'm set up in the car, he returns my items and closes the door. I wait until he's in the driver's seat to ask, "Why are we leaving so early?"

"I'm hoping that we can beat the festival set up. Also, I want to arrive at the store around nine when they open. We can buy you and Arden skates and go skating."

He takes his coffee and sips it before starting the engine. "Did you bring me croissants?"

I open the box and give him a butter croissant.

"Hmm."

"What is it?"

"Your mom made this batch," he complains.

"How do you know?"

He shakes his head, takes another bite, and washes it down with another sip of coffee. "Yours are fluffier on the inside and crispier on the outside."

"That's not true," I argue.

He sets the cup on the cupholder, leans over, and kisses me on the cheek. "It is, but I won't tell her. This will be our secret."

I sigh and turn to look at Arden. "How are you, handsome boy?"

"Otay, Hadey."

"Are you ready to go to Portland?" He nods and shows me his Orca, Oscar. "We are."

"Did he have breakfast already?" I turn back to Mills.

"Yes, we woke up early. He might fall asleep on the drive to Portland."

I don't know about Arden, but I definitely fall asleep. We arrive at the sports store right as they are opening the doors and manage to find a pair of skates for Arden in record time. He's excited to skate like his dad.

Mills insists that I buy a pair for me too and that takes a little longer. We have to go to another store because they don't have any skates that I like and are my size.

As we leave the second sports store, Mills calls the ice rink nearby to rent it, but the manager says he needs to do it at least a week in advance. Instead, Mills drives to Mount Tabor Park where we decide to spend some time.

"Maybe next year I'll move to one of those apartments," I say, pushing Arden's swing.

He loves to be on the swing as much as I do.

"You're planning on searching for a job here, in Portland?" He asks, raising a curious brow.

"I'm not sure," I answer honestly. It's a thought. One of the million I have often about my future. There's the one where he and I live together with Arden. Well, that's more like a dream. I don't know what I'm going to do next because I hate that Arden and Mills won't be a part of that next step, but that's life. "It's one of my options. There are too many factors that will decide where I can go. My resume is still circulating on several websites so I'm hoping to do a few freelance jobs that might land me something more permanent next year."

He looks at me intently. I wish he would talk more than a few sentences and ask a lot of questions.

"What are you thinking?"

"You're already making plans for next year, and I still can't make any decisions about my future," he says, staring at the apartment building I showed him. "I don't see myself anywhere. Most of my brothers know what they'll do after the stipulations allow us to leave Oregon. Vance is just as lost as I am, but that's because he's had a rough couple of months. I don't even know what I'm going to do. Going back to play might end my career and leave me using a cane for the rest of my life. But if I retire now, what am I supposed to do with the rest of my life?"

"Buy a hockey team, and I'll help you," I joke.

"There's that option. We could bring it to Portland. We'd be close enough to Baker's Creek that we can visit our families but far enough that we don't have to deal with the gossip."

The idea sounds perfect, but it also brings thoughts I don't need—thoughts of me, Mills, and Arden—a family. He places his arm around my shoulder, pulling me close to him and placing a kiss on my temple.

"Maybe in a year, we'll be in a better place, and I can ask you on a date," he whispers.

I look up at him, and he doesn't wait for a response. He crushes his mouth to mine, a frantic, possessive kiss, filled with all the lust we've been ignoring. I am about to cling to him when I hear a tiny voice saying, "Hadey!"

We pull apart. My brain fogged by the desire and the sweetness of the kiss. I've missed his lips so much. Mills's eyes are locked on my mouth. They shine with lust. As much as I'd love to continue with that kiss, I turn my attention to Arden. "Sorry, sweetie," I apologize, going back to push his swing.

"When he turns sixteen, I'll be sure to interrupt him when he's with his girlfriend."

I laugh, and Arden laughs with me.

Chapter Eighteen

Mills

MY SELF-CONTROL IS MELTING like the icecap on Mount Hood. I should drive immediately to her place and drop her off. Instead, I propose we go to lunch because being with Arden and her feels just right. It feels familiar. She fits perfectly with us in a way I never thought any woman would fit in my life.

After eating, I drive us back to Baker's Creek. Our normal route is closed by barricades. Every weekend Main Street is closed for the festival. I have to park in The Lodge's parking lot which is almost at full capacity.

"People are going to know I was with you all day," Hadley groans. "I don't have the energy to deal with them."

"I'm dropping you by the main door. I'll park the car in the back. Text me when you're on Main Street so I can start walking home."

"You don't have to do that, I'm just whining. It's good for business, you know. Mom's bakery is going to be swamped tomorrow. They'll be asking questions and she'll make up some story while I'm in the kitchen baking up a storm."

"That's..." I don't even know what to say. "You have a wide imagination."

"Funny that you think I'm joking. Let's not forget that next week it's the Pastry Festival. That means people will be at our booth trying to talk to me. I can't stop thinking about it. Every second manning the booth is just going to be nosy people asking me too many questions."

I park in the back and kill the engine. The thought of Hadley getting bombarded with questions and mean comments doesn't settle well, so I brainstorm. "Do you need me to pull people from The Lodge to help with the booth?"

She looks at me, a mischievous glint in her eyes. "You could help me."

I stare at her, horrified. "That's not funny."

Her eyes narrow as she stares at me thoughtfully. "Who said I'm joking?"

As much as I'd love to help her, that's a hard no. I can't save myself from the town by throwing myself into the gossip mill. "Sorry, I don't do any festival-related activities. Someone has to be with Arden."

"Great excuse big boy, but Mom can watch him while you and I are tending the booth. You might be able to distract them while they pant after you."

"As tempting as I find this offer, the answer is still—"

She places her index finger on my lips after kissing her finger. "I wouldn't ask if it wasn't important."

I rest my head on the back of the seat and stare at the roof. What is this woman doing to me? Since when do I want to go out of my way for a woman? I grab her hand to kiss the finger she laid on my lips. She's not just any woman. She's Hadley.

"Can I think about it?"

"Thank you."

"I haven't said yes," I warn her.

She smiles that playful grin that hits me right in the chest and sends a charge of electricity to my groin. "But you're considering it, and that means a lot to me."

This is the beauty of Hadley. She's happy enough with the affection and the attention of those she cares about.

My phone rings as we exit the car and I let it go to voicemail. If my brothers need me, I'll be there soon. Anyone else can wait.

"I'll unfasten his seatbelt while you get the stroller," Hadley says.

This moment feels just like the entire day: perfect, familiar. I want this to be my life. When she said she'd like to live in Oregon, I saw all of us together, in a house, near a park with a swing. But I don't let myself dwell on it. She's still young, and I doubt she'll want to be tied to us. I wish I could say fuck it all and enjoy her for the next few months, but we can't even do that. If I fuck this up, I'll hurt Arden and possibly the entire family.

We make our way toward the house. Hadley stops at a couple of places and buys a few bags of kettle corn from one of the booths.

"They should call this the Kettle Festival and not The Kettle Chips Festival," she protests, opening one of the bags. She grabs a fistful and eats it all at once.

"For such a small mouth, you can certainly fit a lot there."

She grins, glances at my crotch, and says, "You have no idea." She hands me the second bag, which actually has kettle chips. "Here, Arden can have some later."

"Where are you going?"

"Home," she answers as she squats to meet Arden's eye. "Thank you for letting me spend the day with you, baby boy. Be good to Dad, okay?"

"Otay. Bye, Hadey."

She leaves so quickly it feels like she's running away from us. This might be an omen of what's to come. She'll leave one day and leave us behind. I look at Arden and let out a frustrated breath. I don't know how to act around her or how to protect our hearts. I want a lot more than just a friend who helps me take care of my son. As we walk toward the house, I come to the realization that she might be helping us, but she's taking a piece of my heart every time I see her.

When I get home, I check my phone. There are three missed calls from Margaret and one voicemail.

"I want to see Arden. You can't stop me."

I don't allow myself to worry since she has no idea where we are, but I can't help but wonder why she's constantly fucking with my life. I put her out of my mind as I take Arden out of the stroller. "Later, we should try your skates, so why don't we take a nap?"

"Hadey readz."

"Sorry, sport. She went home."

"Home with Hadey?"

I hear the motor of the stairlift, thankful for the distraction. "Look, your uncle Beacon is coming down the stairs."

"Bacon," he yells and pushes himself down.

I set him on the floor, and he runs toward my brother. Beacon sets him on his lap, and they start going up and down the stairs.

"It's not a toy, Beacon," I call out as they are heading back upstairs for the second time.

"I don't have anything else to do. My physical therapist forbids me to do anything else today. Plus, G went to Portland to pick up her cousin and his family."

I arch an eyebrow. "She drove?"

"Nope, Vance is using the helicopter. We couldn't convince him to let them use the airstrip."

"Why not?"

"He only said, 'fuck no.' Vance is moody or maybe he can't handle us. One of these days he's going to pack his things and leave the town—before the eighteen-month stipulation. If you ask me, we should chain him to a chair until the end of November," he jokes, I think.

In some ways, Beacon understands Vance more than anyone else.

Chapter Nineteen

Mills

I FOLLOW my normal routine for the rest of Saturday. Nothing changes, except, I feel incomplete. It's as if I have a cold and everything is odorless and tasteless. I used to be content with my life and now, I need Hadley's voice, her scent, and her presence around me for it to be full and happy. Around nine, Beacon sends me a text.

Beacon: *Come to the bar.*

Mills: *I thought you were with Grace and her cousin.*

Beacon: *We are with them, at the bar. It's almost a party. You should come over.*

Mills: *I'll pass.*

Beacon: *Fine, but don't blame me if Hadley goes home with someone else.*

Fuck no. If she's going to go home with someone, she'll go with me. Not that I'm going to go and drag her out like a caveman. I make sure Arden is sleeping before I leave. When I arrive at the bar, I hear a very familiar laugh and my eyes find Hadley right away. She's next to a tall guy, the one I'm guessing is trying to take her home. I march toward her. She's wearing a pair of skin-tight jeans, the neckline of her blouse plunging low. She looks beautiful. She always does but tonight she is glowing. My heart beats faster, my length presses hard against the zipper of my jeans. I want her.

I move behind her, glaring at the man that she's flirting with. He glances at me and smiles.

"You must be an Aldridge," he says, extending his hand. "Zeke, nice to meet you."

I stare at his hand, confused. What the fuck? How does he know I'm an Aldridge? Why is he flirting with Hadley? I notice belatedly that the guy next to him is holding his hand while speaking to Beacon who finally notices my arrival.

"Mills is shy. Have some manners, brother."

"Mills Aldridge." I shake his hand, glaring at Beacon.

Beac makes the introductions. "This asshole is Mills, my brother. Mills, you already met Zeke. Next to him is his boy toy, Ethan. Z calls him husband for short." The guy glares at Beacon while shaking my hand, which Beacon decidedly ignores. "The bubbly pixie is Hannah. The guy glued to her is Alex, her husband. Next to him is Tucker and the redhead next to Grace is Sage, who happens to be Hadley's cousin. Did I forget anyone?"

They say in unison, "It's great meeting you."

"Nice to meet you all." I wave at them.

Drew, the owner, comes to speak with Hannah and then takes our order. His brother is married to Hannah's sister. Alex is the one who orders food for all of us to share, and everyone asks for soda.

When he gets to me, I feel weird asking for a beer, so I take a coke just like Hadley.

I enjoy myself while we chat about many things. They ask some questions about my career. It's been a long time since I have had a conversation with adults who aren't my brothers or employees. I think we all need to have a life outside the house. I'm glad that we're bonding and becoming a family, but we have to do things outside of the six of us.

Eventually, the conversation switches toward Hadley.

"So what exactly is it that you're doing?" Sage asks. "If you send me your information, I could connect some of my clients with you."

Sage is a web designer. Maybe Hadley is trying to do something similar to that?

"I manage a few social media accounts and do some branding consulting. If they need me to check why they're not getting enough traffic on their social media or post for them because they are too busy, I'm their person."

We haven't talked about this in-depth before. I make a mental note to ask some questions about her freelancing later.

"We should link our website," Sage proposes. "It'll drive some of my clients to your site and vice versa."

"Thank you, that would be great!" Hadley answers and I feel the relief in her body. She's a lot more relaxed than she was before.

"Of course! I can't believe you didn't contact me when you had that issue. We could've given you a hand. Ethan and Hannah own a media conglomerate. They know people."

Ethan reaches out for his wallet and gives her a business card. "If you need anything, call me. I might be able to get you a job."

I want to hug her by the waist and pull her closer to me. I want to insist that she's staying with me, that she doesn't need anything, that I can take care of her. The bright smile on her lips reminds me of my place. She'll be happier with a job she loves in a place far away from Baker's Creek. If given the opportunity, I'm sure she'll just drive away without looking back for another ten years.

The conversation shifts toward Sage's daughter, Mae, who is staying with her grandparents. Sage's grandmother is the nice lady who owns the bookstore next to the bakery. I didn't know Hadley was related to her though. No wonder she goes weekly for story time and comes back with the new books for Arden.

A couple of hours later, Grace and Beacon start saying their goodbyes. I don't want to leave but everyone else is beginning to get ready to do the same. I offer to walk Hadley to her house. I leave Beacon to walk slowly on his crutches with Grace and match Hadley's pace instead. Maybe I can steal a kiss before I have to go home.

"You should walk with him. I'm fine," Hadley says.

"You're starting a business," I say, ignoring her comment.

"I actually started it almost at the same time I arrived," she answers. "It's more like a freelance gig. I'm still unsure if it's going to become a business."

"So what do you prefer, a job or to get this business off the ground?"

We arrive at her house before she answers, and instead of saying, "Goodbye," I say, "Invite me in."

I want us to talk more about this business. The one that might let her work from anywhere in the world. Not only that, I want to kiss her. I'm done restraining myself. If she allows me, I want more.

Once we're inside, I shut the door with one hand and pull her by the waist with the other. "Someone should give me a medal for keeping my hands to myself."

Her eyes flutter shut. She inhales sharply before opening them again. "You think it's easy for me?"

I set a finger under her chin and tip it up, so our gazes meet. "Can I kiss you?"

She sets her hands on my chest. "Since when do you need permission to do it?"

"Since it'll be the prelude for more. I won't be able to stop myself. I'm going to devour your mouth and then," I lean in close to murmur in her ear. "I'll fuck you senseless."

She grabs the back of my neck and crushes her mouth against mine. There's no sweetness to this kiss, only desperate need.

Hadley slides her hands down my chest and works my jeans open. She pulls my shirt up, interrupting our kiss only long enough for me to push it over my head and onto the floor. My chest rises and falls as she traces the ridges of my muscles with her well-manicured fingers. I'm burning. It's been too long without sex, and the feeling of her small hands on my skin is driving me insane.

"Had, babe, we've been foreplaying for way too long."

She giggles. "That's ridiculous," she says, dragging the zipper down. She pushes my jeans over my hips, and my hard-length springs free.

She cocks an eyebrow, brushing her fingers along my dick. "The things we can do with him."

"Are you planning on having a playdate with my cock?"

The glint in her eyes and that smirk tell me everything.

"We'll see, Aldridge." She licks her lips.

"What do you have under that red blouse?"

She tilts her head toward the staircase and I rid myself of my shoes and pants before following.

"You haven't answered."

"Like you haven't been peeking at me all night," she scoffs.

"Was I that obvious?"

When we enter her bedroom, she turns on the low lights of her room. They're barely enough to see by, but it's enough for me to watch her as she unfastens her jeans and loosens her blouse. As she moves her hips, stripping seductively. She pulls the red fabric over her head. I'm not surprised that she's braless. I've been staring all night at her hard nipples, almost cutting through the blouse.

My cock jerks as she pushes her jeans down, her eyes firmly on mine. I'm hypnotized by the curves of her body, and that tiny piece of black lace covering her pussy.

"Lay on the bed," I order.

She laughs. "Who told you you're in charge?"

"You are in charge," I concede. "I'm here to make you feel like you're in fucking heaven while we sin because that's what you deserve. I will make you scream because that's what you and your body want."

I don't wait for her to do as I say. I lift her with one arm and set her on top of the bed. Her mouth opens slightly. "Can you let me take care of you?" I whisper in her ear, dragging my teeth along her neck.

"Please," she moans.

"We can play all you want after this first time." I hook a finger under the lace and pull down the panties. I drag my finger along her slit until I find her small opening. She shivers when my tongue makes contact with her clit. I'm doing it fast enough, so I push her close to the edge, so she gets wet. She's panting, pulling my hair. When I stop, she glares at me, "Why? I'm so close."

"I want to be inside you when you come for the first time," I say.

"I never come with penetration," she says winded.

"You've never been with me," I claim, but then I realize I'm missing one big detail. "Fuck."

"What?"

"Condom," I say. "I'm celibate."

She points at her nightstand. "First drawer."

"You're prepared?"

"It's a long story I don't want to discuss right now," she says, reaching for the condoms.

She opens the foil and is about to roll it along my length when I stop her.

"Why not?"

"If you touch me, this is over before we start it."

"We wouldn't want that," she says, handing it to me. She props herself on her elbows as she watches me roll the condom. "You have too many rules, Mr. Aldridge. I thought you'd be a lot more laidback."

"You thought about my sex etiquette, Ms. Heywood?"

"That's not what I meant."

I part her legs, holding my cock. I place it right at her entrance. "You can show me what you meant later. Right now, I have to have you."

Slowly, I sink inch by inch inside her. She feels so fucking incredible. She's a different kind of woman. A woman who listens to me, keeps up with my family, and brightens my day. I can't explain what I feel for her because the insatiable need to devour her increases as I'm closer to her. There are so many feelings floating around us and inside me. Most of them are unexplainable and unknown. All I can say is that she feels like coming home.

Her eyes never leave mine, and I can feel our hearts beating together, connected as we are. I thrust hard, fast, seeking her release, wanting to drink her pleasure. I'm so close, but I refuse to come until she does. I feel her shaking, trembling, and moaning as she squeezes my length. My orgasm hits its crest soon after and I take her mouth at its peak.

It's not a sweet kiss. I'm branding her. Possessing her. Making her mine.

And by doing so, I'm making myself hers.

I STAY at Hadley's place until three in the morning. I go through the back door and jump the small fence to the mansion, trying to avoid the front gate and the cameras. You'd think that I tried to break into the bank with the way I'm being tackled before I can take three steps.

"Call the boss," one of them says while the other one ties my hands behind my back.

When I look up, three guys are staring at me, plus the one on top of me. Fuck, when did they place this kind of security around our house?

"My name is Mills Aldridge. I'm on the list," I try to joke. Neither one of them moves.

Vance and Grace, who are part of the high intelligence security company, arrive a few minutes later.

Grace looks at her phone and grins. "You were right. It was Mills."

"Can you let me go?"

"And you set yourself on fire," Vance says, shaking his head in disapproval. "I told you not once but twice that you should stay away from *her*, and what did you do?"

"The only thing I did was try to come into my house, and your—these men attacked me," I complain. "What the fuck is wrong with you?"

"Dad set up the security detail," Grace explains to me. "We're just making sure that the place is safe."

"You could've told me. Can you release me, please?"

"Not only does he not tell us why he's just coming back home, he's jumping the fence. We have a gate, you know," Beacon says on the other side of the line.

"I was trying to be silent."

Grace takes out her pocket knife and cuts the ties. She reaches for my hand and helps me stand up. "The next time you do this, text Vance and Beac."

"There shouldn't be a next time," Vance says with that low warning voice that scares half of the town shitless. "What's the plan? Arden loves her. Things go south, and he's going to experience his first heartbreak. Are you ready for that?"

"You should have a little more faith in Mills," Beacon says over the phone. "He's hooked. Do you think he's going to let her go?"

I want to take the phone from Grace and smash it against the floor. They have to be shitting me. "Can we not discuss my life as if I'm not here?"

"As I said, if any of you ends up crying, I'll kick your ass." Vance turns around and leaves.

Grace shakes her head. "He doesn't know you."

Even though I didn't grow up with my brothers, Beacon and I have been hanging out since he graduated from high school. I would meet him in New York City where he was going to college. Sometimes, he'd fly to visit me. I met Grace eight, maybe nine years ago. It's a little sad that a friend can say something like that about my brother, but what does she mean by that?

"What does that mean?"

"You protect Arden from everything and everyone. You wouldn't get close to Hadley if you thought it'd hurt him. Also, we know Hadley adores your son."

"You're assuming a lot."

"No, I know what I saw tonight. You guys couldn't stop looking at each other or touching each other. Beacon and I agreed that this is the first time we've seen you happy. She makes you smile."

"I just don't know how this will end."

"It doesn't have to end."

It's easy for her to say that. Grace and Beacon have been friends since they were toddlers. They've loved each other since forever. Hadley and I...we just met.

"Is it practical?" I ask.

"Falling in love is never practical. It's magical. You open your heart and let it flow, the same way you let oxygen inside your body."

"It's not that easy."

"You Aldridges make it too complicated." She shrugs as she opens the door. "You don't want to accept it, but Hadley already owns your heart, and you know what they say."

She's talking nonsense. Grace is part of the happily ever after club. She doesn't understand that all Hadley and I can have is *happy* for now. We don't have a future. I humor her anyway.

"What do they say?"

"Once an Aldridge hands over his heart, it's forever." She shrugs again and I know we're thinking the same thing.

I'm so fucked.

Chapter Twenty

Mills

NOTHING CAN PREPARE me for the assholes I call my brothers, so I plan to sneak out of the house early with Arden. We head to the coffee shop first, where I get my usual latte and a hot chocolate for him. The bakery is empty when we walk over, much to our surprise. Then again, I've never been in here at seven a.m. on a Sunday.

"Good morning," Paige greets us and takes a paper bag from the three-tier display case that's next to the register. "We got something special for you."

"You spoil him."

"Hadley thought it'd be a good idea to make cake pops out of the cakes we didn't sell yesterday."

"Hadey!" Arden claps his hands. "Whes Hadey?"

"Is she in the back?"

Paige nods.

"Can we see her?"

She glances around the shop as if making sure that no one is listening, before leaning in. "Listen, I'd prefer if you keep things strictly professional between you two. People are starting to talk."

People are always talking. I want to tell her that things between Hadley and I have changed, but I don't know if that's something we're going to address anytime soon. I wouldn't care either way, but what does Hadley want?

"I wan my Hadey!" Arden screams so loud everyone turns to look at us.

Hadley comes running out of the kitchen, alarmed. Her light brown hair has a coat of flour, matching the tip of her nose. "Is he okay?"

"Hadey!" He looks at her with so much love.

"Hey, baby." She comes from behind the counter and lifts him from the floor. "What's happening?"

"He's fine," I state, not telling her that her mother was trying to send us away.

"Go home," Arden says, clinging to her neck.

"Can we go home?" She corrects him, kisses his temple, and looks at me. "Why don't you guys go to my place? I should be done in about thirty minutes."

Her mom exhales so loud it feels like there's a windstorm inside the bakery. I can tell that the woman hates my guts. "You can leave. We have everything under control. Just think about our earlier conversation."

Hadley's attention goes to me. "He's not going to let me go, is he?"

I shake my head apologetically.

"I'll clean myself at home, then. Can you come over to the break room so you can help me with my things? Mom, can you put two croissants, a cinnamon spice muffin, and some cookies for me in a box."

I head to the break room to pick up her sweater and her purse, take the box of goodies from Paige, and leave the store not before saying, "Have a good rest of your day, Paige."

This would be a good time to ask if her mother hates me. I don't. There's a big chance that someone will listen to our conversation and spread a version of it around town. We walk toward Hadley's place in silence. Once we're inside and the door is locked, I give her a peck on the lips. "Hi."

"Hello yourself. I wasn't expecting to see you today."

No one will keep me away from seeing her today or ever. "We're trying to avoid my brothers."

"Why?"

"It's a long story," I yawn.

"You didn't get much sleep, did you?"

If only she knew how my night went.

"It was fine. Why don't you tell me what's happening with your mom?"

She shakes her head as she places Arden on his highchair. "Have you had any breakfast?"

Arden shakes his head.

"I'll make us something," I volunteer, setting everything that I'm carrying on the table. I hand Arden his hot chocolate. I offer the latte to Hadley.

"This is yours," she says, trying to refuse it.

"We can share."

She takes a sip, kisses my cheek, and goes to the fridge. There's a small container that she opens and gives to Arden. "Here, have some blueberries while we get breakfast ready."

When we're in the kitchen, I take her into my arms and kiss her senseless before greeting her properly. "Morning, beautiful."

"Morning," she says, breathless.

"Why did your mom tell me to keep this professional?"

"As predicted, people saw me with you yesterday, and they are assuming that I'm trying to get me an Aldridge."

"They are wrong. I'm trying to get myself a Heywood," I correct her, kissing her on the cheek and running my lips along her jaw. "How do you want to handle *us*? I don't care if the entire town learns that I'm crazy for you, but I don't want this to affect you or your parents."

She places her hands on each side of my face and says, "You're perfect."

"I'm everything but, babe. Tell me, what is it that you want us to do?"

"Can I think about it? Mom is having a hard time with Dad's situation. She doesn't like that we depend financially on you guys. She suggested I look for a job. I don't think she understands that if I stop working for you, everything she has right now will disappear."

"It wouldn't," I say. "If you have to leave, I'll make sure she keeps the nurses, the therapists, and the employees."

"That wouldn't be fair to you."

I don't argue with her, but I circle back to the fact that she wants to stay. She shouldn't stay against her will or out of obligation to us.

"Do you want to leave?"

The lines between her brows deepen as she stares at me. "What kind of question is that?"

"I don't want you to stay with us because you feel obligated."

She glares at me and turns around to open the refrigerator. She pulls things out of it and shoves them on top of the counter.

"Hadley."

She pokes my chest and says angrily, "I don't want to speak to you right now. You can be so fucking infuriating."

I stare at her. What did I do?

"Sorry, I didn't mean to overreact but it sounded like you don't care if I don't stay," she says with a calmer voice. "Mom always sounds like she doesn't want me around while simultaneously making me feel bad for not staying."

"That wasn't my intention."

We cook together in silence. When we sit for breakfast, she finally speaks. "Listen, I'm not concerned about what the town says. I'm more worried about him." She tilts her head toward Arden, who is fighting with his fork and the scrambled eggs. "I don't know what the end game is. I want to think that he and I share a special bond. It'll be devastating if I can't see him ever again when things are over. Mom is pretty intuitive. When I walked into the bakery this morning, she said, 'You slept with *him*.'"

"No wonder she almost kicked me out of the bakery when she saw me."

She laughs. "I don't understand what's upsetting her. The town will move on with the next order of business. It'll probably be Henry's twins or Vance being the grouch of the town, or maybe Beacon's bandmates hooking up with someone in town."

"Have they?"

"No, but everyone is trying to sleep with them. One of them will succumb, and that's when the town will forget that I exist. If not, I don't care anymore. Do I want us to go public?" She looks again at Arden. "I care more about his feelings."

This is why I am falling so madly in love with her. She's beautiful, intelligent, and funny. I can spend hours talking to her and I can tell how much she loves my kid.

"So we keep it under wraps for now," I state. "For him."

"I think it's for the best, don't you?"

Sure, but for how long? I'm new to relationships. While in high school and college, I concentrated on school and practice. All I wanted was to become a professional player. There's one thing my brothers don't know; my father threatened my hockey career. If I didn't finish a college degree, he'd make sure no one in the hockey league would draft me. Dear ol' Dad was a powerful asshole. He paid people off just to fuck around with us. I didn't have time to entertain a relationship back then.

I don't know when it'll be a good time to come out and tell everyone we're together. I want to do it now, but I don't want this to affect Arden or Hadley. Why is life so fucking complicated?

"If you feel that's the best, we'll do it your way," I agree. "Since it's Sunday and everyone at home is busy, why don't we try the ice rink?"

"Let me take a shower. Should I wear a jacket?"

"I think you'll be fine with a long sleeve shirt and jeans."

"Okay, but you get to clean him." She points at Arden, who has scrambled eggs on his head and blueberries smeared on his cheeks. "Good luck!"

Chapter Twenty-One

Hadley

WE SPEND what feels like hours in the ice rink. My time is divided between my ass hitting the ice and taking pictures of Arden. I love the latter the best. The smiles he gifts me with while he's pushing his little ice walker are more precious than gold. In a couple of weeks, he won't be using it because Mills wants him to find his balance. It's pretty cute when Arden marches, imitating his dad. My favorite part is his giggles every time I fall.

"His face is too red. Do you think we should go back home? I can warm up milk and make some instant hot cocoa. He can have a snack or a nap. Maybe both."

Mills looks up at the big clock on the left wall. "Yeah, we've been here for almost an hour. I think this is more than enough for today."

He picks up Arden and skates toward the edge. Mills makes this look so easy. I try to do the same, and I start wobbling.

"Let me take off his skates, and then I'll come and help you."

I ignore him, and of course, my ass hits the ice again.

He slides with grace toward me, places an arm on my back and the other under my knees, and picks me up. "I told you to wait, woman."

"Stop bossing me around. I can do it myself."

"Sure. The next time we do this, I'll bring you with a helmet and a pillow tied to your beautiful butt. If anyone is going to crack it, it's me, not the ice." He winks at me.

"You wish."

"Baby, if only you knew all my wishes, you might never talk to me again." He places me on the bench, helping me take off my skates. "I'll put the skates in the locker room. Give me one second."

"Did you like skating?" I ask Arden as I'm putting my boots back on.

He nods and yawns, placing his hand over his mouth in the most adorable gesture I've ever seen.

"I'm sweepy."

I take him in my arms and press him against my chest. "We're going to get something warm to drink, and then we'll read a story, okay?"

"Otay."

"Are you ready?" Mills asks, taking Arden from my arms.

"He is more than ready," I brush some of his blond hair away from his tiny face.

"You know what would make this perfect?" he asks.

"Hot cocoa?"

"I was thinking, a little girl," he says.

"What are you talking about?" I stumble on the words just like I almost do on my feet.

He shakes his head. "Never mind, I was thinking out loud."

"Whatever you're thinking, don't," I order.

What is wrong with this man? I'm telling him that we have to take this slowly, and he's already thinking about more kids?

My mother is freaking out because I might be dating an Aldridge. I haven't confirmed or denied the allegations but Mills visiting me at the bakery was enough evidence. We can't just spring our relationship to his son. I adore the kid, but what if things go wrong? I'm usually an optimist, but this relationship doesn't scream long-term. I already dated a wealthy asshole. Well, Randall wasn't rich, but he comes from a wealthy family. Mills is not an asshole, but he might become one after we break up, and then what am I supposed to do with all the love that I have for him and Arden?

Mom is right. I am making a big mistake. When this is all over, I will have to gather my dead heart and leave the town unemployed and alone.

Mills leans closer to me and kisses my cheek. "We'll take it slow," he promises, and try as I might, I don't believe him.

AFTER ARDEN IS TUCKED into bed for his nap, I tiptoe outside the room. Mills disappeared while I was reading a story to answer a call from one of his brothers. When I reach the house's first story, I find Blaire, Leyla, Sophia, and Grace sitting around the table. There's a teapot, teacups, and cookies on the table.

It feels strange. "Are we having a tea party?"

"We have been since these two can't drink anymore," Grace says, glancing at Blaire and Leyla.

She points at the empty chair next to her. "Why don't you take a seat? Would you like to have some tea? If not, there's juice, water, beer, soda...you name it. We will bring it for you."

I yawn, stretching. "I have to head home."

"She's trying to escape," Sophia says, cocking a brow. "Listen, either you sit and talk, or we'll follow you, and we'll still make you talk."

"Finesse is not one of your strengths?" I joke.

"Not when I'm two thousand months pregnant, my children keep pushing my bladder every two fucking seconds, and you're making this difficult."

"That makes sense," I say, afraid of the pregnant lady that might be about to snap my neck because I'm...difficult apparently.

I decide to sit. "So, what's all this about?"

"You and Mills, when did you two start dating?"

"We're not dating," I state.

Sophia laughs and rolls her eyes. "Denial. We know you two are together. We want dates. They matter."

"I told you it was last night," Grace states.

I try to divert them with another question. "Where did you get that strange idea?"

Leyla is the one who says, "I have people. They talk a lot with the right incentive. You two were cuddling last night at the bar." She glances at Grace. "Then, there's *the incident*."

I narrow my gaze, staring at Grace. Is there something I'm missing? Do they have cameras in my house, and they recorded everything that happened last night?

Instead of making a bunch of nonsense assumptions, I ask, "What incident?"

Grace stares at the ceiling before bursting into laughter. Whatever this incident is, it must be pretty funny because she can't stop laughing.

When she composes herself, she finally speaks, "We caught Mills sneaking into the house earlier today. It was pretty funny."

"I've no idea what you're talking about," I try to play dumb. I want to ask what she means by catching him. And why are they all laughing?

"Mills left your house around three in the morning. He tried to avoid the gate and the outside cameras by jumping the small fence between your house and ours. It triggered the alarm." Her eyes dance with laughter. I swear she's having more fun than I did last night. "The security team tackled him down. It was very entertaining."

"The video is a blast," Leyla agrees. "We should ask Beacon to replay it for Hadley."

"That's not funny," I protest, relieved that they aren't talking about a sex video.

"When you're stuck with those six men, everything they do is funny," Sophia argues. "Give it a month or so, and you'll understand what we're saying. In a couple of months, you'll be drinking wine while watching them do something dumb. It's their nature."

"I miss wine." Blaire shakes her head, then turns toward me. "We knew you two were going to end up together. I understand if you have to hide it from the town—"

"We don't understand it," Sophia interrupts her. "But we will support you if you choose to do so. Personally, I like you, and I think you fit perfectly with Mills and Arden. However, it's about how you feel. I also hope that you trust us enough to be there for you because being with an Aldridge is not easy."

"She gets the easy one," Leyla says. "He's a simple guy with fewer hang-ups than the rest of the guys. Still, he's an Aldridge."

Grace places a hand on top of mine. "What they are trying to say is, welcome to the family and our sisterhood. Also, the Aldridge boys are a world of their own. They like to know everything."

Blaire nods. "They do."

"You do too, bitch." Sophia glares at her.

I have fun with them when we hang out. A few days ago, Grace came to my defense when the Marys were bitching at me. I trust them more than I trust the rest of the town. There's not much I can lose if I tell them what's happening with Mills.

"The relationship is new to both of us. I don't know where it's going, but I want to pursue it just as he does. We're doing it slowly and keeping it under wraps for the foreseeable future because of Arden, not the town. I love him, and the last thing I want is for him to be confused or hurt because of something we do."

"This is why we like you and why you fit so well with us," Blaire states. "You make sense, and I agree. Even though we put Arden's well-being above everything, none of us thought about it the way that you two do."

I've liked these ladies since I met them. As I spend more time with them, I'm glad that we're becoming friends. Also, they support Mills and love Arden a lot. If I am honest with myself, I'd like to be a part of this fun, loving, messy family.

Will that even be possible?

Chapter Twenty-Two

Mills

WHILE HADLEY IS READING a book to Arden, Pierce asks me if I can join him and our brothers for a moment. They need to talk. I want to avoid him and my brothers for another five to six months but it's impossible when you live with them. I follow behind him, and my stomach drops when we pass the kitchen and continue outside the house.

"Where are we going?"

"Beacon's underground place," he answers. "As I said, we need to talk."

"Can you give me a preview?"

He picks up the pace. I do the same.

When we arrive at our destination, everyone is in the living room, beer in hand and sitting quietly.

"What happened?" I ask, bracing myself for something terrible.

Did someone fuck up and the lawyer caught them?

"So, you're doing the nanny," Pierce starts.

"Asshole, did you seriously bring me down here just to ask a stupid question?"

"No. We all knew it'd happen. It was just a matter of time," Henry states. "The when is pretty important. Was it last month, and we just caught you? Or was it last Wednesday? Or perhaps we're making shit up, and you haven't done it at all."

"Give it up and just pay me my fucking money," Beacon says. "I said this weekend, didn't I?"

"What did he do?" I ask to no one in particular.

They respond with a shrug.

"I swear I'm going to break that back again. Let's see if anyone will be able to put you back together," I threaten him.

"Boys, don't start to fight," Hayes says, exasperated. "You touch his back, and you and I will have a problem. It took me hours to piece him together. Now, would you say that you had sex with Hadley before last Monday?"

I point at the five of them and warn them. "I swear I'm going to kick your asses"

"You can try," Beacon offers.

"Why are you obsessed with when it happened?" Then I stare at Beacon. "Why do they owe you money? Did you bet about it, asshole?"

"We made it interesting. Try living in this town without much mobility, and you'll find ways to have fun," he says as if his accident absolves him from being an idiot. It doesn't.

"You bet on me having sex with Hadley," I run a hand through my hair and exhale loudly, annoyed as hell. "What kind of asshole does that?"

"I'm not an asshole. I was just bored. Plus, you denied that you liked her. Like we couldn't see you drool every time you saw her. I knew that when I set you guys up on a non-date, you wouldn't be able to resist."

"What do you mean setting us up on a date?"

"Last night, remember? We could've hung out at Tucker's home but you wouldn't have come. If we moved the party to the bar, I knew both of you would feel more comfortable."

"You set that up?"

He nods, seeming pleased with himself. "You're welcome."

"That's cheating," Henry protests.

"It would've happened. You were already out of the running. It was between Pierce and me," Beacon argues.

I look at Vance, "What did you bet?"

"I didn't. I was hoping you wouldn't be stupid." He shrugs.

"We're keeping this on the down low. Arden doesn't know about us, and I want to keep it that way for a while. Can you be discreet?"

They nod in agreement.

"If I stay the night at her place, can your people not attack me when I'm trying to get back into my house?" I glare at Beacon. He looks at Vance, who nods, and then he says, "We'll make a plan so that what happened last night doesn't happen again. So are you two together?"

I bring them up to date on what Hadley and I decided. Once I'm finished, Beacon says, "Sage and Grace were talking about the town. As you know, Sage lived here for a few years before moving to Seattle with Tucker. I asked if she knew my father or anyone in the family. She didn't. She suggested I ask her lovely grandmother, but I don't want her to know that we're looking into our father's life in Baker's Creek."

"I thought you had people digging around," I say.

"We do, but they haven't uncovered anything we don't already know. What if Hadley helps us?"

If he thinks she's going to do it willingly just because I ask, he's wrong. Besides, I have no idea how much he made just for setting up last night's date, but I'm not helping him. "You can talk to her."

"You could do it too," he suggests.

"If you want her to help, ask her directly," I insist.

He nods. "Fine, we'll make this our next project."

BEACON DOESN'T WAIT to ask Hadley for help. It's right after Arden is in bed that we're all hanging out in the living room when he suggests she become our spy.

"What are you looking for?"

"Who did he hang out with? Did he have friends?"

She looks at him. "I could ask Mom or maybe my great aunt. She has a bookstore where some students hang out after school."

"What if we ask her to carry some of our chocolate and candy in the bookstore?" Sophia asks, who apparently can't think of anything else but shoving the Aldry's products down everyone's throat.

"No." Hadley almost glares at her. "You're selling them through Mom. If you give that to the bookstore, we're going to lose those customers. I'm working on convincing her to stay open until five, while I convince her to leave the bakery early and trust her employees."

"We could set up cameras inside the shop," Vance suggests. "She can watch what's happening at the shop from the comfort of her house."

"You can do that?"

He looks at Beacon, who nods once.

"Then we keep all our products with your Mom," Sophia

concedes. "That said, can you ask around? We just need to know who he was dating before he left for college."

"That's pretty specific," Hadley looks at me, wondering if they're serious.

I explain to her about Dad's letters, how he left one for each of his sons and one for our significant others. We don't receive them unless the lawyer thinks we're worthy of them. Only Blaire, Hayes, Henry, Pierce, Leyla, Grace, and Beacon have received theirs.

"What do they say?"

"We don't know," Henry answers. "We're waiting for everyone to receive their letter. However, Leyla received two. The one we read gave us a clue that he was in love once."

"Why did you open hers?" Hadley asks curiously as she pulls out her phone. When I glance, she opens her notes application and starts typing. "Why didn't Sophia get a letter?"

"I did," she states. "Mine was generic. I don't think William knew about me or he would've left one for me."

"Did yours have a clue?"

"What are you typing?" Sophia answers the question with one of her own. "And no, there wasn't any clue."

"We need to gather all the evidence. I have to remember the details, so I ask the right questions."

"It's safe to say she's on board," Grace concludes. "If you need to run any background checks, we have the system to do so. There has to be someone in town who knew him well."

"Why is it so important?"

"It might tell us why he never came back unless it was the one week during summer that he had us all get together" I answer.

"I remember those days." Hadley smiles fondly. "One of you would come to the bakery and order an entire box of croissants and a cookie. He'd sit on one of the outside tables and eat them. He always gave me a cookie, too. He was super nice."

We look at each other and grin when we all say, "Carter."

"Mom used to say he reminded her of Mr. William before he left Baker's Creek," she states.

"What if your Mom broke his heart?" Blaire asks conspiratorially.

"Ew, she was like seven or eight when he left for college," I tell her.

She flinches. "Oh, I didn't know that. Sorry. Maybe some jaded woman who stayed behind without her William? Wouldn't she be either hating on you or trying to take care of you?"

"Someone who left right behind our father," Pierce suggests.

Vance says something that we never considered. "What if we're looking for a her and it was a he?"

Beacon answers, "You're expanding our search. Good. It might be plausible and the reason why we're not finding shit. It's in your hands now, Hadley."

Chapter Twenty-Three

Hadley

"YOU DON'T NEED to work every day, Hadley," Mom says when she enters the bakery.

I didn't go to sleep last night. Mills left around almost three-thirty so I took a shower and came straight to the bakery. I arrived thirty minutes before her so I'll probably be too tired by noon. Maybe I'll take a nap at the same time as Arden does.

"I like doing it, Mom. How is Dad?"

"He's doing a lot better. I don't know how I'm going to repay you."

"It's nothing," I say, kneading the dough for the bagels. "Can I ask you a question?"

"Yes, I'm still against your relationship with the Aldridges. More if you're hugging them in the middle of a bar."

I burst into laughter. "Mom, I'm a grown woman. If I kiss Mills in the middle of Main Street, it's my business."

"They're going to be talking about you."

"For sure, and I'm going to ignore them the same way I've ignored them my entire life. However, that's not what I wanted to ask."

"Just be careful. I told you with Randall, and I'll tell you again, men don't buy the cow if they get the milk for free. Now, if you end up pregnant, that man is going to take that kid away."

I love my mother, but she blows things out of proportion. She forgot to add that if he knocks me up, I'll be the talk of the town. She should have a little more faith in me. I'm on the pill, I have condoms. I know how to take care of myself. If anything fails, I wouldn't just leave my kid to be raised by his father. We would find a way to co-parent the baby.

It's useless to tell her she's blowing things out of proportion.

"I wanted to ask if you knew who William Aldridge dated while he lived in Baker's Creek," I talk fast before she interrupts me with her nonsense.

She goes to the sink to wash her hands and then looks at me. "What?"

"You said you knew him. Who was he dating at the time?"

"I was a kid. If your grandmother were alive, she'd know it."

"Did William have any friends?"

"Christopher," she answers. "He lived in Happy Springs and came to visit him every day. They went to school together. That was back when they only had one high school for both towns."

Did he have a girlfriend in Happy Springs and that's why we can't find her in Baker's Creek? If we figure out who this guy Christopher is, maybe he can tell us more about William.

"What was Christopher's last name?"

She shrugs. "How would I know?" Her eyes study me closely. "Why do you want to know?"

"His sons want to know more about him. They're curious about his childhood," I respond, hoping that my answer satiates her curiosity. "If they want to find any yearbooks or information about him, they have to go to Happy Springs?"

"I don't know if they have anything in the new school," she continues. "There was a fire when I was in junior high. That's when the towns decided to build a high school for each town."

Well, that doesn't help me much. The guys could try to look for a guy named Christopher in Happy Springs. He might have more information about their dad.

"Hadley, I feel like you're tangling yourself with those men, and you'll end up crying when they leave you behind."

Wow, she makes it sound as if we're all getting involved.

"Did anyone cry when William left the town?" I ask, turning her question back on her.

"The few that knew him missed him. He wasn't the same after that day, though. I don't think I ever saw him smile again."

"Maybe he didn't want to leave."

"He always said he had to do it. That was the deal between his mother and father. He'd stay until high school. Then he'd follow his destiny."

For a person who didn't know much about William, she sure has a lot to say about his past.

"What was his destiny?"

"Take over the businesses, and then the town. Not that he took care of us after he left. Up until last year, The Lodge was falling apart. The factory almost closed. He forgot about his duties, and his sons will do just the same."

They wouldn't just leave this town behind. Baker's Creek is in better shape than it was when I was in high school. The brothers keep renovating the buildings, adding new features, and supporting everyone in any way they can. I bet if I hadn't come home, but they had seen my parents struggling, they would've helped. That's why Leyla bought the goats from Mom. She plans on returning them once Dad can take care of them.

They added new equipment to the park. I'm pretty sure they took my bench, but they won't admit it. I might just carve my name on the new one.

AT DINNER TIME, I bring up my conversation with Mom.

"We knew about the high school," Beacon says, fixing a taco. The guy prepares the best tacos I've ever tried in Baker's Creek. "Which was a big roadblock. There aren't any yearbooks in the Happy Springs library."

"He had a friend named Christopher."

"Any last name?" Vance asks.

I shake my head. "It's a small town. What are the chances that there are more than ten Christophers around your father's age?"

"She has a point," Mills agrees with me, then he adds. "Maybe tomorrow you can ask if she can describe Christopher."

"That wouldn't work much because the guy is going to be shorter, with gray hair, or maybe bald," Vance corrects him.

I tell them everything Mom told me.

"Maybe he loved this town so much, and it hurt that his father dragged him away from it."

"What if this town is his true love?" Henry asks. "At eighteen, the only thing he cared for was the town, and he had to let it go. People like William and I focus a lot on the material. We get attached to it. Thinking with his logic, he brought us back to put it back together and treat it the way he would've if he hadn't been stopped by our grandfather."

"Fuck, after a year, I have learned how to speak Henry. He

makes fucking sense," Pierce says, staring at Henry. "You are twisted if those are your priorities."

Henry kisses Sophia and then her belly. "I was. My priorities have changed a lot since I came here."

"So we leave it alone?" Pierce concludes. "We figured out the mystery of why we're here?"

"No," Beacon says. "We know one of the motives—maybe. There are more, though. The guy was in love. We just need to figure out who she was and why he left. I feel like I need to learn about it to get closure."

"Closure?" Mills asks.

"Yes, my life turned upside down because my father lost someone. I want to know that she was worth my broken back, my career, and my patience."

Grace gives him a strange look.

"Fine, it was worth getting those assholes into my life and most of all because I finally let myself be with my woman. Still, I need to know, okay?"

Grace kisses him.

I adore watching them. He's so loud while she's so quiet. It's like he speaks for her, or she speaks through him.

"What's our next move?"

"I'll ask Mom more questions. If Sage were still talking to her father, I'd suggest him. He's almost the same age as William."

"You could ask your mom if they were the same age," Mills suggests. "If they are, we can ask your great aunt for his yearbook. We can say we want a copy to "preserve our father's memories" or something like that."

The conversation moves toward The Lodge. Sophia wants me to take a look at the social media of Aldry's and see about starting one for The Lodge. Once we finish eating, Mills, Arden, and I go for a walk around the property. I show Mills my favorite spot, which is next to the ice rink arena.

"You like to mark everything, don't you?" He points at a tree that has my name.

I shrug. "Don't be surprised if you wake up with my name written with a permanent marker on your chest."

"As long as you don't use a pocket knife, I'll be fine with it."

After Arden goes to bed, he proposes that I stay for the night. His offer is tempting, but I don't think it's a good idea to do it just yet. It'll confuse Arden and that's the last thing I want to do.

The other reason is me. I don't want to fall for this guy so fast that there's no net to catch me.

Chapter Twenty-Four

Mills

BEING WITH HADLEY IS EASY. We set up a routine where I end up sleeping half of the night in her bed and the other half in my own. We convince Easton to set up a gate in her backyard so we can go in and out of her house with more ease. Everything and nothing changes. Hadley continues to take care of the children. However, she's not an outsider. Everyone has embraced her as if she's part of the family. I want her to be a part of me. We have passion, fire, and blissful content.

Neither one has defined any of the emotions we feel for the

other. I know those feelings run deeply inside my heart and my soul. We can spend hours at night talking about nothing and everything. We make love before we fall asleep for a couple of hours in each other's arms before I have to leave her place and head home.

Some days I feel like time passes so fast I can barely be with her. Three weeks after our first night together, Sophia gives birth to the twins, Thayer and Holton.

The house becomes a battlefield just as I predicted, so I start to spend more time at Aldry's. Hadley starts to stay at the house overnight, in case Sophia and Henry need help—or to help me soothe Arden. This new change is affecting his sleep pattern. Having four infants and a toddler in one house is close to a three-ring circus. By week three, Hadley begins to move her clothes to my closet.

She stops going to the bakery because she can't physically wake up before six in the morning anymore. Waking up to help my brothers and sisters-in-law is exhausting us both. I started using Sophia's driver the day I almost fell asleep driving to Happy Springs.

Beacon's bandmates help us with the barn, and some days, they also help with the babies. I swear Arden wasn't this complicated when he was an infant. Though, to be fair, he didn't have four other babies crying at the same time.

"Hadey!" I cover my head with the comforter when I hear Arden scream too fucking early in the morning.

When I feel his feet bounce on the bed and Hadley's naked body rubbing against me, it hits me what's happening.

"Oh god, we forgot to lock the door last night," she mumbles.

"Hadey is with Daddy!"

"In case anyone was wondering, the news of the day is, Hadley is sleeping with Dad," I hear Beacon say so loud I'm afraid they can hear him all the way to Portland. "Rookie mistake. You two should learn to lock the door. Come on, sport. Let's head downstairs to see what we're having for breakfast. Your dad and Hadley will come downstairs once they wake up, okay?"

"Otay."

"You owe me, Mills."

When I hear the door close, I push the blanket away. Hadley is in a fetal position hiding under the crook of my arm with her eyes closed.

"Are you trying to make yourself invisible?"

"Is it working?"

I kiss her temple. "Nope, but you're so fucking adorable."

"He caught us. We've been so careful, and he caught us."

"You can't block the sun with one finger. It was bound to happen at some point, Had."

She finally opens her sleepy eyes and yawns. "What are we going to do?"

"We don't hide from him anymore. It's okay that he learns that I'm in love with you."

Her eyes open wide. "What did you just say?"

"It's okay that he learns about us."

She rolls her finger. "No, after that."

"That I love you?"

She nods a few times.

"Are you surprised? What's not to love? You're brilliant, patient, loving. I couldn't help myself. Even if I wanted to," I say, rolling her under me. Right as I'm about to thrust myself inside her, someone knocks on the door. "Time's up. Come downstairs now."

Hadley cups my face. "For what it's worth, I love you too."

I rest my forehead on top of hers. "It's good to know that I'm not alone in this. We'll work this out with our boy, okay?"

She stretches her neck and kisses my lips. "Okay."

I'M NOT sure what it is with Arden, but after finding Hadley and me in bed, he's been clingy with her. They are adorable, but I want to know why he's acting like that. Does he think that Hadley is no longer his? Should we explain to him that we're together? Hadley bought a book called: How to Bring a New Partner Into Your Child's Life. We're reading it slowly, but is it the right time to say, Had and I are together?

I don't know what's going to happen in the future. Hadley still has plans for her future. I am contemplating the possibilities. Three people have suggested that I buy a hockey team.

Owning and managing a team will make it easier for me to be with Arden. That's as far as I can think of the advantages. It's Friday when Vance and Beacon call us to another family meeting. They've found a lot of information based on what Hadley has dug up about Dad.

"We haven't found a Christopher," Vance says. "However, do you know who used to live in Happy Springs until he turned eighteen and left for college?"

We all look at him expectantly.

"Timothy J. Pelletier," he answers.

"And we care about Timothy because?" I ask, trying not to snap at him, but for fucks sake. This Hardy-Boys-Nancy-Drew search with Hadley is getting fucking ridiculous. We could be doing our nightly walk, but instead, we're paying attention to the worst detectives in the history of the world.

"You're not curious about the J?"

"John, Johnson, Joshua… who the—"

"I swear, Henry, if you drop an f-bomb, I'm going to punch you so hard you'll need surgery to reconstruct your bones."

"Babe, calm down," Hadley says, kissing my cheek.

"Cam down, babe." Arden says from her lap.

Everyone laughs because it's adorable, and this is precisely why I believe a little girl will complete our small family. She'd be just like her mom. Not that Hadley, Arden, and I are a family, but I'm more convinced every day that we belong to her.

"His name was Timothy Jerome Pelletier," Hadley says.

"Jerome Parrish?" we all repeat.

He is Dad's lawyer—the one who is making sure that we abide by the stipulations.

"You investigated him, and you didn't know that he was from Happy Springs?"

Beacon glares at me. "I only knew about his first name. He's been living with his college roommate forever, and he took his last name before he passed the bar exam. It didn't seem important at the time. I didn't dig about his past because honestly, who cares where the dude came from? I didn't think it mattered until Hadley's great aunt mentioned him."

"What do you mean she mentioned him?"

"She said, 'You can ask, Tim. He was a couple of years younger than your dad, but they were friends.'"

Someone should tell Beacon that he doesn't need to imitate voices when he's telling a story. Also, that his imitation of his grandma's voice sucks.

"When we asked her where we could find him, she told us he visits us often. He goes by Jerome now."

"Do you think they were together?"

"We don't know, but we'll find out the next time he visits us."

"Does he have a family?" Hayes asks.

"Four sons, two daughters. His husband owns Parrish Holdings. Again, I knew all that. I just didn't think it was important until today."

"You think Dad was in love with him and…" I don't finish because there are so many reasons why my grandparents could have stopped this, and I'm sure it'll make me hate them more than I already do.

"We'll have to wait, but in the meantime, we're going to dig up more information about him," Vance says. "It might not be him, but there's a link. What if this Christopher guy is real, but we can't find him?"

I feel like we're yet hitting another roadblock. Do we want to know more about his past? Does it really matter? The more we find out, the more I wonder about who he really was. Why did he stay away from us? Was he afraid of loving us? When I take Arden to bed I wonder if Dad was afraid that he wouldn't be able to love us, or that he would shape us into the bitter man he became.

Maybe we'll never find out and we should just let him rest in peace.

Chapter Twenty-Five

Hadley

THERE'S NEVER a dull moment when I'm at the Aldridge house. And since I'm here every day, naturally none of my days are dull. Arden and I take a few breaks from the noise from the twins and the chaos in the house by going to my house or visiting Dad, who adores him. He finally calls him Papa Rick. It took me some time to work on his R's, but he is doing a lot better. At last, he's no longer calling Dad a dick.

I shouldn't complain much about the chaos that is the Aldridge Mansion. It's fun to live there even when there's always a baby crying or one of the guys whining about some nonsense. Since I can't work at night anymore, I use the time when Arden and the other babies nap to work on my business. It's not big, but I'm earning enough to support myself and help Mom with whatever the bakery needs that she can't afford, like new muffin pans, utensils, and a new logo for the bakery.

It's around noon. Arden is already taking his nap when Mills arrives.

"What are you doing?" He asks, kissing me on the lips. It is ridiculous to say that I love how domestic we are, but I do.

"I'm about to do some work. If I'm lucky, I can write a report before Carter or Arden wake up."

"Where is Machlan?"

"Blaire took him to the pediatrician." I sigh, thankful that I only have two of the youngest Aldridges. "I don't know what we're going to do when Sophia and Henry's parental leave ends, and I have to take care of the twins too."

"We'll cross that bridge when it's time, Had," he says, kissing me. "Let me make myself something to eat, and I'll keep you company while you work."

"What are you doing here so early?"

"It's the perfect time to hang out with you. I don't have to worry about anyone that might interrupt us. Maybe if Arden is still asleep, we could play," he says suggestively.

I laugh. "We just played during our shower earlier, Mills Aldridge."

"It was so long ago. I need it again."

I open my computer, check my email, and there it is, the email that I was hoping for when I first quit the Troopers in March. It's August. It's too late to get a response from all those applications I sent. I have a job that pays amazingly, it comes with great benefits —and I get to stay at home with the most wonderful boy in the world and his cousins.

"What is it?" Mills asks as he takes a seat next to me.

"A job," I mumble vaguely. "It's a job offer. It pays six figures—double what I made before."

"Don't they need to interview you first?"

"They did, back in April," I answer. "I went through the entire process. The same way I did with a lot of other companies who had open positions but didn't bother to send me an email saying 'sorry you're not who we're looking for.'"

His expression flattens. He runs a hand roughly through his hair. "You never told me about it."

"What was there to say? I'm interviewing, but all these teleconferences are blending in with each other. The only thing they are teaching me is that I'm still unemployed. It didn't seem relevant. I stopped searching for a job once you guys offered me one."

I suck on my lower lip as I think about this position. It's perfect for me. I could give these guys a two-week notice, search for an apartment, and move out just in time. It takes me a second to remember that I can't just pack up and leave.

When I look at Mills, he says, "You should take it."

My heart cracks. His words settle under my skin. He's telling me to go? I don't know if I want to go. I don't know what I want, but who I want is him and Arden. Yet, he doesn't care if I leave. "What?"

"The job. It's a great salary, and the benefits are almost as good as the ones we offer at Aldry's. If I were you, I'd ask them for executive housing while you find a place to stay. They can afford it."

My mind is reeling. "You want me to go," I clarify after I find the energy to speak again.

What about us?

"Of course," he chirps, fully unaware of the panic he is causing. His expression shifts and goes carefully blank. His voice says I'm happy for you, his posture doesn't give anything away. "It's the chance of a lifetime. You said it, they're doubling your salary. If a team came today and offered me twice what I was earning with the Orcas, I'd sign immediately."

"You would leave without thinking of those you leave behind?"

"But that's the difference between you and me. I have to stay because a lot of people count on me. You don't have anyone like that, though. Your parents will be fine. I'll make sure they are taken care of, okay?"

I feel numb. It's like he punched me in the gut, pushed all the air out of my lungs, and hit me on the head so hard I don't know who or where I am.

"Are you going back to work today?"

He shakes his head. "No, why?"

I shut down my laptop and start putting it away. "This is something I have to discuss with Mom."

"Hadley, there's nothing to think about, you should just go. It's not about your parents, it's about you."

"The logistics." My mind is still swimming, so I just force out the first words that come to mind. "We have to figure the logistics out first, okay?"

He smiles and nods. "That makes sense. Let me know if there's anything I can help you with. I can get you the moving company or have Vance fly you to Portland."

I nod and turn away, hiding my face from his line of sight. He's pushing me away with such friendliness. It's so different from what Randall the asshole did, but the pain feels the same. He obviously doesn't care that I'm leaving. He's acting like he's being supportive but all he's doing is pushing me away. We are dating, aren't we? Why is he talking about this like we're friends and not lovers? I can feel myself start to shake with the realization that it's over. Maybe it never even started.

I take a deep breath and focus on keeping my voice steady. "Arden is taking a nap. His snack is ready in the fridge. Carter will need a bottle and a diaper change when he wakes up. Text Leyla when he's up so she can wrap up her day and come back home."

I hear him go still behind me. "Hadley, are you okay?"

"I got a job offer. Why wouldn't I be?" I answer, before running out of the house.

I DON'T RUN to the bakery, but I walk fast enough to reach home and text mom that we need to talk. With her new employees, it's hard to have a conversation at the bakery. They are all ears and pretty good at communicating what they hear to the rest of the town.

Once we're both in the living room, I explain to her about the job offer.

"You have to take it," she insists, much to my surprise. "There's nothing in Baker's Creek for you. You were born for greatness, sweetheart."

Why does everyone want so badly for me to leave?

"I thought you wanted me to take over the bakery," I mumble.

"That isn't what *you* want to do, though. I didn't raise you to believe that your destiny is the bakery like Mom did with me. This place is your legacy, and maybe when you retire, you'll come back to take over. You're so smart that you'll figure out a way to keep it going without you having to be here."

I want to say, "It sounds like you don't need me."

I'd always known I didn't fit in Baker's Creek, but I never expected that the people I love would actually tell me I didn't belong.

I thought I did, with Mills and Arden. We fit so perfectly together. Mills understood me since the first night we spoke, and I love his son as if he were mine. And yet, his first response was to tell me to leave.

"Is this going to be a problem because of the Aldridge boys?" Her voice brings me back to our conversation.

Of course she's concerned about her financial situation. My parents still have a long way to go. Fortunately, I have enough money in the bank to help them. "No. I'll pay them for terminating the contract early. The employees are staying with you. I'll send you a monthly check to pay for Dad's expenses. The settlement was big enough that I can afford it, I just wanted to save money in case I didn't get a job."

The words are coming out so easily, anyone would think that I'm fine. Not even my mother can sense how broken I'm actually feeling.

"When are you leaving?"

Wow Mom, way to jump to conclusions. "I have to accept the offer first. After that I'll figure out the logistics. Though it sounds like everyone is okay if I leave right now."

"Your dad is going to miss you," she says.

But not her? I thought we were closer than this. That she'd care if I left. "I'll come by when I know more."

"Hadley, this is a good opportunity for you. Don't waste it," she says, just in case I wasn't going to accept the job.

"I get it, I get it. Stop nagging me."

I arrive home and lock the backyard door in case Mills considers visiting me. I reply back accepting the offer and indicating that I'm available immediately. It only takes two hours to coordinate with the human resources director to have a job. They booked me a flight for tomorrow, which is Tuesday, and I'll stay at a hotel while I find a place. I start on Wednesday. I will be working from the Seattle offices since I don't have a visa to work in Canada. They'll be applying for my residence in four weeks. They didn't explain the reason behind the waiting time, and I didn't bother asking

Since I don't know which Aldridge I should give the news to, I go to the house around seven, when I know dinner is over and they will be either hanging out in the living room or by the firepit. Or they could be watching the sunset as they do every day—it's a tradition they started after Beacon's accident. I always meant to ask what it means.

As predicted, they are by the fire pit—all of them.

"Hadey," Arden runs toward me, excitedly. I'm going to miss his voice and that big smile that brightens everything around him. I'll miss everything about him.

"Hey, sweetie," I hug him tight, knowing this is the last time I will have him in my arms. Of all the goodbyes I've ever said in my life, this one is the hardest. If I could, I'd take him with me.

"Where have you been?" Sophia asks. "Your guys seemed lost without you."

"We weren't lost," Mills protests and looks at me. "What did you decide?"

I smile, kiss Arden's forehead, and say, "The Vancouver Orcas offered me a full-time job as their social media director."

"You work for us," Henry barks. "Pierce, remind her that we own her little ass until the end of the year."

I pull out a check from my back pocket and hand it to Pierce. "This is everything you spent on my father. If you need more, let me know."

Pierce frowns, staring at the check as if it's a strange artifact he's never seen in his life. He turns to look at Henry.

"Who is going to help us with the little demons?" Henry's stunned voice sounds almost the same as Pierce's face looks. Henry glances around the group. "Am I the only one who wants to stop her? Mills?"

I want to snort but I control myself. Mills wants me to go.

"We can't keep her here just because it's convenient for you, Henry. We don't need her. I can take Arden with me to Aldry's every day."

Henry stares at him and nods. Then he looks at me and says, "You'll be missed, but I guess this is where you leave."

I nod back. "Thank you for everything you've done for me. If there is any way I can repay you, please let me know."

Everyone hugs me and wishes me luck. Everyone except for Mills, that is, who is seated until I hold out Arden and say, "Can you take him?"

He doesn't answer, but he rises from his seat.

I hug Arden one more time, trying to absorb all the goodness inside him. I'm going to miss him so much. I wish I could beg Mills to let me see him once in a while, but I know I can't because I have no legal rights. I'm just the woman who took care of him for a few months. I hold the tears threatening to break free.

"Arden, it's time for me to go. You be good for everyone, okay?"

He nods and gives me a sloppy kiss on the cheek. I'm all too aware of the sharp pain in the middle of my chest. It's over. The dream didn't last long, but the agony may stay forever.

"Thank you for everything," I say to everyone.

"Good luck, you're going to do great things," Mills responds, taking Arden away from me.

I expect a kiss or a hug— something that gives me a clue that he cared for me. Instead, though, he turns around and heads to the house. I pivot to leave before the tears can begin to roll. When I get to my house, I lean against the door and start to cry.

Chapter Twenty-Six

Mills

IT'S BEEN ALMOST two weeks since Hadley left. I haven't slept for shit. Between my son waking up every three fucking seconds crying for her and my body not being able to get comfortable because she's not beside me, I'm going fucking nuts.

No one understands why I didn't ask her to stay. She deserves to have her own life and dreams. Baker's Creek isn't her future; I can't make her stay in a place she hates just because my son and I love her. I forbid them to mention her name. I'm hoping that in a month or so, Arden will forget about her.

My brothers and sisters won't let me forget about what I did, though. They keep nagging me about her departure and asking questions every time they have a chance. At least they don't do it in front of Arden.

Tonight, we're in the underground game room, or as Beacon likes to call it, his house.

"Why did you let her go?" Henry asks. I swear he's asked this for what feels like a million times. Can he just let it go?

"You don't force people to stay with you," I say, because that's what he did with Sophia. He forced her to move to Baker's Creek with the excuse that he couldn't do anything without his assistant. But I refuse to submit Hadley to a life that she hates.

"You're a fucking idiot," he says. "She was here willingly. Or ——let's not even focus on her physical location. You could've continued dating her even when she left. There are phones, planes, and even computers to reach your loved ones at any time. It's not like you're going to find someone else to love. She's it—the love of your life."

"Once you give your heart away, you'll never get it back," Hayes reminds me. "We Aldridges only love once."

"That's a stupid theory," I claim.

Beacon glares at me, shaking his head. "If you were going to do something this stupid, you shouldn't have involved your son. Arden is just as broken-hearted as you are! You should jump on a plane and head to Seattle. If not for you, do it for your son. They love each other. She's the closest thing he has to a mother, and you just pushed her away without even thinking about him. You're a selfish bastard."

"I'm thinking of him. What's going to happen when we break up? She's going to leave him. She left him."

"No. You pushed her away," Vance finally speaks up. "I was there when she gave you the news. You literally packed up her shit and shoved her onto a plane. When she came to say goodbye, you shut her out. You're a selfish coward who only thinks about himself."

"She wanted to leave. You weren't there, you didn't see how excited she was by the offer. I didn't push her. I told her to do what's best for her."

"Did you give her an option to decide what "best" is for herself? How about saying something like, 'I know you've been waiting for this opportunity, but I love you, and even if you leave, I want us to stay together?' That is what you say. You don't tell her 'I'm taking my love away and fuck you for considering your options.'"

"That's not what I did."

"I'm done with your fucking shit. If you need anyone to fly you to Seattle, find someone else. I'm not helping you fix your shit show." Vance leaves the game room.

Beacon whistles. "I've never heard him speak that much, ever."

My brothers stare at me. I decide to leave rather than explain myself to them. I don't think any of them will understand.

THE FOLLOWING DAY, it's my turn to pick up the pastries. "Good morning, Paige," I greet her

She hands me the white box I've come to associate with mornings. "Thank you," she says.

"For what?"

"I thought you were going to stop her," she answers. "It wouldn't be fair for her to stay here. You'll be leaving soon, and she'll be stuck in this place where there's nothing for her. The night she came to say goodbye, my husband tried to stop her, saying he'll miss her. I had to push her out of the house before he got all sentimental."

"Well, you two will miss her."

She shakes her head. "We will, but we never tell her that. I always make sure that she knows we don't need her. Look at what happened the last time I told her that. She came back."

"You don't want her here?" I ask.

"I want her happiness more. This town isn't what she needs."

"You can't decide that for her," I protest, and then it hits me. I did just that—I made the decision for Hadley.

She didn't listen to me. She left because I made her feel like she doesn't belong. I never gave her the option to choose, I had already decided what was best for her. Not that it was better to let her go. It is too fucking painful not having her with me.

An unfamiliar angry fire flicks in my chest. I'm angry at myself. My heart is pounding as the full weight of the realization sinks in. I didn't do her any favors by telling her to go and acting like an aloof asshole. How am I supposed to fix this mess?

On my way to the house, I see Grace, who I know helped Hadley with her move.

"Hi, have you talked to Hadley lately?" I ask almost desperately. My voice is dire.

She glares at me.

I blow out a slow breath. "You can say it, I fucked up."

"It's what every Aldridge does—you guys just don't get it. Stop making decisions for other people because you feel like we need someone to save us. It was her who came and saved you."

"I know. Where is she living now?"

"I let her live at my place while they figure out her work visa. My brothers are visiting her often so she doesn't feel alone. She's doing fine. She'll be fine."

When she mentions her brothers, I remember that one of them is a pilot. "Do you think you can help me with something?"

"Tell me what your plan is and if I like it, I might be able to give you a hand."

Chapter Twenty-Seven

Hadley

MY LIFE in Seattle is very different from my life in Denver or Baker's Creek, but I'm adjusting. I fly to Vancouver at least three times a week, unless there's a game in another state. Instead of babysitting one toddler and four babies, I have to take pictures of an entire team of men who behave like toddlers.

Instead of posting to their individual accounts for them, my two assistants and I are teaching the boys how to come up with engaging content for themselves. The goal is that by the end of the year, I'll be only coordinating the entire operation without having to travel or post for the guys. I'll just be in charge of the team's account.

Am I happy with my new job?

No.

The idea of starting my own business and growing it exponentially was exciting, a lot more exciting than my current job. If I hadn't been pushed away by my mother and the man who claimed to love me, I would've taken my time to explore my options. But this job was the best excuse to quickly leave a place where I wasn't wanted.

A few perks of living in Baker's Creek for those months were connecting with my cousin Sage and meeting Grace. Grace allows me to live in her gorgeous house, and I visit Sage when I'm in town. You lose some people; you win many more. On Saturdays, I go to the farmer's market. That's the closest thing there is to a festival here. Is it pathetic to miss Baker's Creek?

I haven't spoken to Mom since I left. More like since she shoved me out of her house. She's called me a few times in the last week, but I've sent her to voicemail every time. I text her with the excuse that I'm out of town, or that my cell phone service is crappy. I need just a little more time to forget how shitty she made me feel. I know she loves me, but sometimes she treats me like a stranger.

My phone rings when I'm on my way back from the farmer's market. It's Grace.

"Yeah?"

"Where are you?"

"Almost home. Did you come to visit me?"

She laughs. "Like I can just leave town. Do you know what it takes to get permission from Lawyer-with-a-big-stick-in-his-butt to leave? A miracle. You have to be either in danger, losing a family member, or promising him your firstborn."

I laugh. "That's such a lie."

"Fine, he doesn't request your firstborn, but it does take a lot to convince him to let you leave the state for an overnight trip. He's so strict. You're a few minutes late, and he wants to sell all the properties."

"He can't be that strict, but I'll believe you. So, tell me, what is happening in Baker's Creek?"

"Nothing much," she answers. "It's a regular Saturday. There's a festival. Beacon and Vance are betting on who's going to be washing the barn for September."

"The entire month?"

"Only weekends," she answers. "I hope Beacon wins, because if not, I'm going to have to help him. I love the animals, but I'm not a fan of cleaning up after them."

I'm tempted to ask about Arden or Mills. I miss them both so much.

When I approach her house, I notice a car that I don't recognize. "Hey, should I be worried that there's an SUV in your driveway?"

"No," she answers. "It could be my brother or my parents. They might be checking on you or the house. If it's my brothers, don't make eye contact and try to keep them away from the sun. They are harmless unless you overfeed them during the day."

I laugh, opening the garage door and parking my car. "You're insane."

"They say worse things about me."

"Let me get these things inside, and I'll call you later."

"Or you can just leave me on the phone while you carry the stuff in. I promise you won't even notice I'm here."

I'm guessing she's trying to see who dropped by her house. I place the phone in my back pocket and walk toward the trunk when I see Mills standing beside the SUV. Arden is in his arms. I come to a complete stop and stare at them.

"Hadey?" His voice is so soft, almost afraid. His head rests on Mills's shoulder. He looks at me shyly.

My legs want to move, my head is stopping them. I press my lips together, almost biting them. Hoping that maybe that'll stop the tears from flooding my eyes.

"Hey, sweet boy."

"Hi," Mills greets me.

I nod at him. "Why are you here?"

He looks down at Arden. "He misses you a lot."

"Oh," is all I can say to him. I want to reach out to Arden, but I can't. If I reach out, I won't let him go again. Not ever.

"I thought you wanted the job," he starts. "For some reason I can't comprehend, I thought, if she gets the job, then she won't want to be with us anymore. I didn't want us to be the reason you turned it down. The way I handled the situation was stupid. What I should've said is, "I love you and if you think that's what you need to do, we'll be here waiting for you." The thing is that if we got serious, the lawyer would've made you stay in Baker's Creek. I don't want to force you to do that."

My heart stutters. He loves me? Then what happened the day I told him about the email? He just said a million words that made no sense. Is he going back to: This is for your own good? "What does that mean? That the lawyer will make me stay?"

He swallows hard. "It's one of the stipulations. If we get into a serious relationship during this period, our significant other must follow the will's stipulations. Including the one that says we can't leave the town unless Parrish gives his consent. I don't want to limit you."

A few tears roll down my cheeks. But I need more before my heart forgives him and my legs make it all the way to where he stands. "What are you trying to say?"

He smiles. "I'd kneel, but Hayes told me I can't do that or I'll damage my knee." He pulls out a red box with golden letters. *Cartier* it reads. When he opens it, there's a sparkling solitaire ring inside. "If I do this—if I say the words, I'm asking you to come back with me, and you won't be able to leave town. Are you okay with that?"

His green eyes meet mine.

"Why would you do that?" I ask. "Why would you propose?"

He lets out a nervous breath. "Because I love you with all my heart. Because being without you is the most awful feeling I've ever experienced. Because you understand me more than anyone in the world. You've become my friend, my confidant, and my—" he clears his throat and spells, "L-o-v-e-r."

His words are beautiful, but my heart took a beating. Should I just trust him and forgive him? "You gave me nothing when I showed you that email. It destroyed me when you pushed me away. How can I trust that you won't do it again?"

He sighs loudly, blinking a couple of times. "Everything I do is to protect you. I did it because I was scared by how much you mean to me. I didn't want to keep you in Baker's Creek against your will. I don't want to let you go, but I did because I love you."

I let my tears run freely. He's breaking me apart more and then gluing me back together with his words.

"I thought I was doing what's best for you. I wasn't. I destroyed the three of us. We've been lost without you. I want to propose to you because I want us to be a family. Because we belong together. We are yours, Had. Would you do me the honor of becoming my wife and Arden's mother?"

I nod as I'm trying to control the fast beating of my heart. He wants me to be a part of him. He wants us to be a family. "Yes," I say between sobs.

"Yes?"

"I want us to be a family. I don't know how I'm going to do my job from Baker's Creek, but I want to be with you."

He steps forward and takes me into his arms. Arden hugs my neck and whispers, "Mama."

I sob harder. I'd have given anything to be his mom, and now I'll get the chance. "I missed you, baby boy."

"Biss you." he hugs my neck so tight, almost as tight as Mills is hugging me.

"Are you taking me home?" I ask.

"Not quite yet," he answers. "We're spending the weekend with you, and then the three of us are going to Vancouver. There's business we need to take care of on Monday."

Epilogue

Mills

LEAVING Baker's Creek pays off. Not only do I convince Hadley to take my sorry ass back, but I also buy the Vancouver Orcas. I plan on moving them from Vancouver next year. We still have to decide on the new location. It'll be between Seattle and Portland-- it all depends on what is easier for our family and for the team.

It takes us another two weeks to let the world know that Hadley and I are engaged. She needed to coordinate her assistants, hire someone to travel with the team, and discuss her future with Ethan since he had hired her as a freelancer for HANNETH.

Hadley plans on growing her business. She won't be quitting the team, but she might switch from an employee to an external consultant once she's ready to hire more people to work for her. We got married in early September, since neither of us wanted to wait. I wanted her not only to be my wife but Arden's mom. He hasn't called her Hadley or Hadey again. She's his mama now.

As for Hadley and her mom, they're finally talking through their differences. Paige means well, but she has to stop thinking that her daughter is an inexperienced child.

It's almost dark, signaling the time for us to do our nightly ritual of watching the sunset over the lake.

"Why do you guys do this every day?" Hadley asks.

"According to Beacon, while he was in surgery, he had a vivid dream. He was with our brother Carter who stayed with him until he came out of his coma. They were here," I point at the tree and continue explaining, "Sitting there watching the sunset. We believe that Carter's spirit comes every evening to do the same, and we spend those few minutes with him."

She kisses my cheek, and she's almost crying. "That's so sweet."

"It is indeed," A male voice startles my brothers, Hadley, and me.

When I turn around, I see Jerome Parrish watching us.

"Why are you here?" Pierce asks.

"I wasn't invited to this wedding," he says, pulling out two envelopes. "If I hadn't learned that you all are digging for my past, I'd believe you have forgotten all about me."

He looks at Hadley and gives her an envelope. "This is a strange union. A Heywood and an Aldridge together. Back in the day, it would've been scandalous."

"How do you know my father?" I ask, cutting straight to the chase. "You two weren't just a client and a counselor."

He gives me an envelope. "I wasn't anyone. This is just a simple transaction." He tips his hat and leaves.

"This would've been a good time to ask him some questions,"

Hadley says.

"What does your letter say?" Beacon asks, ignoring her comment.

"I thought you weren't supposed to open them until everyone gets one."

"Except if they are generics," Beacon says.

She opens it, frowns a couple of times while reading it, and then hands it to me.

Dear,

I'm sorry that I didn't get to meet you. I hope that you're everything my son and my grandson need. Marie was an extraordinary woman and a great mother, and I think she did a great job with him. I was the one who made him doubt that love exists, but I'm glad he found the woman who restored his faith in love and family.

I only ask that you love him like he deserves and that you are enough to be the mother of his precious son. I hope you build a family that fills your house with laughter and love.

With all my love,
William.

The letter doesn't answer any of my questions. I'm not even sure why he bothered. Or if maybe those letters are another joke. I wanted to believe that the letters he wrote to us have more meaning but reading this letter I'm not sure if I want to read it. What if it's something generic? There's one thing he got right. Hadley and I love each other. We are planning on building a bigger family, so she's no longer taking the pill. If we're lucky, next year we might be holding a precious baby that will have her smile and those big brown eyes I adore.

I hand the letter to my brothers, take Hadley in my arms, and kiss her. She is indeed the perfect woman for me.

"I love you," I murmur in her ear.

"The feeling is mutual, Mr. Aldridge. We might go against nature and Heywood vs Aldridge protocol, but I don't know what I'd do without you and your love."

Dear Reader,

Thank you so much for picking up a copy of As We Are.

Mills is what I called my easy child. When I planned this series, I knew he'd be my break between two angsty books. Hint, Vance is not going to be light at all.

As We are is exactly what I needed to write in that moment. I needed a sweet love story. Which makes this book one of my favorites.

Also, Arden deserve to have an easy transition from Vancouver, to Baker's Creek, to finding a woman who'd love him like her own. That little boy deserved easy too, even when Mills messed up a little.

I know you have a lot of questions, and you wished they were answered here but ... Vance is doing all the leg work and I felt like it was fair for everything to be unveiled.

Is it going to be an easy book? Probably not. Are you going to love it? I totally hope so.

One last thing, if you loved As We Are as much as I did writing it, please leave a review on your favorite retailer, Goodreads, and on Bookbub. Also, please spread the word about The Baker's Creek Brothers among your friends. One of my favorite things about writing is sharing these characters with everyone.

Sending all my love,
Claudia xoxo

Acknowledgments

First and foremost, thank you to God because he's the one who allows me to be here and who gifts me the time, the creativity, and the tools to do what I love.

Thank you for all the blessings in my life.

Thank you Luis, P, A, and S. My family is not only loving but the most supportive one.

Nina, Kelly, and all the team of Valentine's PR. To Kim, for keeping me organized, all her help in the background, and listening to my craziness from time to time.

Hang Le, my longtime friend and my cover artist. She always understands what my books need.

My betas: Erica, Amy, Darlene, Karen, Melissa, Patricia, Caroline, and Yolanda for always responding to my incoherent questions. Their feedback is important just like their friendship.

To Karen, Kristi, Amy, Mary, Dylan, and Jenn for always listening to me while I'm writing.

To all my readers, I'm so grateful for you. Thank you so much for your love, your kindness, and your support. It's because of you that I can continue doing what I do. My amazing ARC team, girls you are an essential part of my team. Thank you for always being there for me. My Grammers, you rock! To my Chicas! Thank you so much for your continuous support and for being there for me every day! Thank you to all the bloggers who help me spread the word about my books. Thank you never cuts it just right, but I hope it's enough.

Thank you for everything. All my love,
Claudia xoxo

About the Author

Claudia is an award-winning, *USA Today* bestselling author. She writes alluring, thrilling stories about complicated women and the men who take their breath away. She lives in Denver, Colorado with her husband and her youngest two children. She has a sweet Bichon, Macey, who thinks she's the ruler of the house. She's only partially right. When Claudia is not writing, you can find her reading, knitting, or just hanging out with her family. At night, she likes to binge-watch shows with her equally geeky husband.

To find more about Claudia:
  website
  Sign up for her newsletter: News Letter

Also By Claudia Burgoa

The Baker's Creek Billionaire Brothers Series

Loved You Once

A Moment Like You

Defying Our Forever

Call You Mine

As We Are

Yours to Keep

September 2021

Luna Harbor (2021/2022)

Finally You

Simply You

Truly You

Always You

Perfectly You

Madly You

Second Chance Sinners Duet

Pieces of Us

Somehow Finding Us

Against All Odds Series

Wrong Text, Right Love

Didn't Expect You

Love Like Her

Until Next Time

The Spearman Brothers

Maybe Later

Then He Happened

Once Upon a Holiday

Almost Perfect

My One

My One Regret

My One Despair

The Everhart Brothers

Flawed

Fervent

Found

Standalones

Us After You

Someday, Somehow

Chasing Fireflies

Something Like Hate

Until I Fall

Finding My Reason

Christmas in Kentbury

Chaotic Love Duet

Begin with You

Back to You

Unexpected Series

Uncharted

Uncut

Undefeated

Unlike Any Other

Decker the Halls

Co-writing

Holiday with You

Made in United States
Troutdale, OR
01/12/2024